Caribbean Island Hospital

Twin docs in paradise!

Welcome to the US Virgin Islands! Home to doctors Matthew and Marcus Oleson. Matthew and Marcus may be twins, but they couldn't be *more* different. Their passion for treating patients and saving lives might just be the only thing that they have in common! Until a surgeon and a nurse burst into their hearts…and Matthew and Marcus find that they have falling in love in common, too!

Escape to the Caribbean with…

Reunited with Her Surgeon Boss

A Ring for His Pregnant Midwife

Available now!

Dear Reader,

Thank you for picking up a copy of *A Ring for His Pregnant Midwife*, which is book two of Caribbean Island Hospital.

I dreamed of this duet a couple of years ago. Marcus and his twin, Matthew, walked into my head fully formed, and I'm so glad I get to share their stories with you.

Alexis, a nurse and midwife, is pregnant and needs to escape all the pain of her heartache in England and the betrayal of her ex-husband. What better way to get over heartache than by starting fresh in a tropical paradise.

Marcus has no plans to ever settle down. He's experienced heartache before and has no desire to ever put his heart on the line again. Until his pregnant friend begs him to enter into a marriage of convenience.

A marriage with an end date seems doable. The only problem is the mutual attraction that Alexis and Marcus feel for one another. And too many heated kisses under the Caribbean moon may mean forever.

I hope you enjoy Alexis and Marcus's story.

I love hearing from readers, so please drop by my website, www.amyruttan.com, or give me a shout on Twitter, @ruttanamy.

With warmest wishes,

Amy Ruttan

A RING FOR HIS PREGNANT MIDWIFE

——

AMY RUTTAN

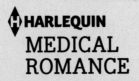

HARLEQUIN

MEDICAL ROMANCE

⊕ HARLEQUIN®
MEDICAL
ROMANCE™

Recycling programs
for this product may
not exist in your area.

ISBN-13: 978-1-335-40920-1

A Ring for His Pregnant Midwife

Harlequin Enterprises ULC
22 Adelaide St. West, 41st Floor
Toronto, Ontario M5H 4E3, Canada
www.Harlequin.com

Printed in U.S.A.

Born and raised just outside Toronto, Ontario, **Amy Ruttan** fled the big city to settle down with the country boy of her dreams. After the birth of her second child, Amy was lucky enough to realize her lifelong dream of becoming a romance author. When she's not furiously typing away at her computer, she's mom to three wonderful children, who use her as a personal taxi and chef.

Visit the Author Profile page
at Harlequin.com for more titles.

For my editor, Julia.

I'll miss working with you. Thank you for putting up with me these last couple of months and helping breathe life into Marcus and Matthew.

CHAPTER ONE

MARCUS WINCED AS he tried to climb out of the narrow bed on his sailboat. He was eight weeks past his transplant surgery, but the incision was still healing.

His new sister-in-law, Dr. Victoria Jensen-Olesen, had given him a clean bill of health, but his body was not bouncing back quite as fast as he would have liked. His brother, Matthew, would say it was because he was getting older, but Matthew was twenty minutes older than he was, so the joke was on him. Marcus was the younger and fitter twin.

In theory.

He winced again and grabbed a pillow to brace his side.

Ugh. Maybe Matthew is right. Maybe I'm getting too old.

He laughed as he stood up.

Truth be told, he was bored out of his mind.

He'd had to take a sabbatical from his work as a physician while he healed, and Victoria had warned him that he couldn't get back to his regular practice until he was twelve weeks postoperative. It felt like an eternity.

Only a month to go.

All he wanted to do was get back to work.

Work kept him sane.

That and women, but since his godson, Jonas, had gotten sick, and Marcus had volunteered to be part of the domino surgery in St. Thomas that would provide Jonas with the kidney he so desperately needed, he hadn't paid much attention to dating.

Not that he ever dated seriously.

He'd made that mistake once before, and once was more than enough for him to learn his lesson.

In his early twenties, Marcus had fallen in love with Dawna, the smartest and most beautiful woman in med school.

He'd lost his heart to her.

When his brother went off to New York to do a residency in surgery, Marcus had followed Dawna to California and taken a post in the emergency department at a hospital in San Diego. He had learned triage and was one of the best emergency physicians on staff.

Marcus had thought he'd had the future all planned.

He was going to have an extensive practice in San Diego, and then he was going to ask Dawna to be his wife. He had carved out this whole life for them. Unfortunately, Dawna had other plans, and he was left devastated when she left him for an uptight surgeon that sort of reminded him of his twin brother.

It had crushed Marcus to lose the woman of his dreams to a man who was so like Matthew, because he'd spent so much of his youth being told by his parents that he should try to be more like his brother.

Instead of sticking around in California and working with Dawna and her new surgeon husband, Marcus headed back home to the US Virgin Islands to lick his wounds, vowing to never, ever put his heart on the line again.

Famous last words. Look at Matthew.

Marcus ignored that thought and slowly got dressed for another day of sitting around and healing.

"Yo! You up, Marcus?" a voice called from the dock.

Marcus made his way out into the galley of his boat, the *Tryphine*, and saw his best friend, Jonas's father, Chase Fredrick, looking down at him from above deck. His friend smiled, but Marcus could instantly tell that there was something wrong with him.

"Chase, it's not Jonas, is it? I thought he was still in Charlotte Amalie?"

Chase nodded and walked down the stairs into the galley. "Jonas is stable, thanks to that amazing surgery your brother and sister-in-law performed. He's taken well to his anti-rejection medicines, and he's due to be released soon,"

Marcus smiled. "Good. I'm glad to hear it. What can I help you with then?"

"You're not back to work yet, are you?"

Marcus shook his head. "Nope. I haven't been cleared to practice yet. What's wrong? Is something wrong with Pepper?"

Pepper was Chase's wife and Jonas's mother, and she was currently pregnant with their second child. Pepper had had problems when delivering Jonas, so the couple was understandably nervous about this new pregnancy.

"Actually, there is something wrong. You know that St. John is having a shortage of midwives, especially midwives that can handle the kind of issues Pepper had previously?"

"Right."

Chase rubbed the back of his neck nervously. "Our midwife, who is from England and who is so phenomenal, is about to get deported."

Marcus's eyes widened. "Deported?"

"Her visa's up," Chase said. "She's helped women like Pepper before and successfully dealt with preeclampsia and sickle cell disease. She's so knowledgeable and Pepper adores this midwife. Completely trusts her and no one else."

"Well, I'm sorry to say that she might not have a choice if her midwife is going to be deported."

"Well, that's where you come in." There was a nervous tone to Chase's voice, and Marcus had a sinking feeling in the pit of his stomach.

"What do you mean?" he asked carefully.

"Well… I don't know how to ask you this since you've done so much for our family already, but I'm desperate. I don't have any other single friends."

Marcus suddenly felt like he was going to be sick and he sat down, bracing himself. "Chase…what exactly are you asking me?"

"Would you ever consider a marriage of convenience?"

Marcus started to laugh at the absurdity of the question. "Be serious."

"I am being serious."

Marcus stopped laughing and cocked an eyebrow at his best friend. "You've been so stressed going back and forth between Ziese Memorial Hospital and home, plus dealing with a pregnant wife. You're obviously over-tired and talking nonsense."

"I'm not!"

"So you're serious?" Marcus asked in disbelief.

"Deadly. I have a clearer head than you, not to mention the fact that I'm younger and better looking."

"That's what I tell my brother."

"And that's what I'm telling you," Chase teased.

Marcus rolled his eyes. "Uh-huh. I would believe what you were saying if you weren't proposing such an insane idea. You can't be serious."

Chase nodded. "I'm being serious. Look, it's the only way I can think of keeping her in the country. You know that Pepper has sickle cell anemia, and this midwife is the best we've seen. I don't trust Pepper in anyone else's hands."

Marcus sighed.

It was a big ask, but he could tell that Chase was desperate, and he knew his friend had undoubtedly thought of everything else before proposing this idea. Chase knew about his past with Dawna, and he also knew that Chase wouldn't have made this big ask if it wasn't his last resort option.

"The doctors in Charlotte Amalie could take care of Pepper, Chase."

"I know, but Pepper is really comfortable with Alexis, and Pepper isn't her only patient. There are others, and everyone loves Alexis on the north side of the island. We can't lose her."

Marcus sighed again. "I don't know. How long would this take? How long would I have to be married to this person?"

"Two years, give or take."

"Two years?" Marcus shook his head. "I can't do that."

"I know it's a long time."

"It's more than just a long time—it's years. Not days or months, but *years*! Can you imagine me married for that long? I have no desire to have a wife or be a husband. Real or imagined."

"Not even a fake husband?" Chase asked, with hope.

"Not even that. Imagined means fake. Not real. No. It's not happening."

"I know you swore off marriage and relationships a long time ago…much to Pepper's chagrin." Chase smiled and Marcus chuckled.

Pepper had been trying for years to set him up with the right woman, and Marcus had managed to rebuff her at every turn. Matthew's late wife, Kirsten, and Pepper had also teamed up for a while, but Marcus just couldn't let go of how much Dawna had hurt him.

You're afraid. That's why.

Marcus shook that thought away. "What does this fake marriage entail?"

Chase grinned. "Just a quick trip down the aisle so that Alexis can apply for her green card. Any immigrant with a pending green card application is allowed to remain in the US until the application has been decided on, which means not only will Alexis be able to stay and see Pepper through a safe delivery, she can also help countless other mothers-to-be while she waits for her green card to be approved. Once she has it, you can get a quickie divorce."

"You know this is fraud, don't you?" Marcus asked dryly.

"Yes, but I'm desperate. Alexis is an asset both to Pepper and to the medical profession. She *deserves* to stay, and I know her application will be approved, so all we're really doing is helping the process along so that she can keep helping women like Pepper."

"Pepper needs to stop reading so many romance novels. I'm sure that's where she came up with this crackpot idea."

Chase laughed. "She's hooked on Mills & Boon, what can I say?"

Marcus stood and sighed. "Does this Alexis person know of this plan?"

"She does, but she's not convinced. Yet. I'm confident we can talk her around to it. Together."

Marcus groaned. "Now, I suppose?"

"You have something better to do? You're on medical leave."

"You're being awfully pushy today, Chase," Marcus groused.

Chase grinned. "No more than usual."

Marcus shook his head and grudgingly finished getting dressed. "You owe me big-time, Chase. Big!"

"I know." Chase climbed up the stairs and

stepped out onto the deck to let Marcus get ready in private, but turned back at the last second, and Marcus could see he was worrying his bottom lip.

"What now?" Marcus asked with trepidation.

"The thing is, she's also pregnant."

"Pepper? I know Pepper is pregnant."

"No, our midwife."

All the blood drained from Marcus's head, and there was a strange ringing in his ears.

Surely he hadn't heard Chase correctly. It sounded like the most absurd thing ever.

"She's pregnant?"

Chase nodded. "Yeah, the father of the child left her and doesn't want anything to do with the baby."

"I can't get involved with a pregnant woman. I'm not involving a child in this kind of…of ruse. It's two years or more before she'd get her green card. It's somewhat acceptable when it's just two consenting adults involved, but she's pregnant and that child will be born into a union that isn't genuine. This isn't right."

"It's not a ruse. She'll get her green card. She just needs a husband on paper for the time being. You don't have to be a father, and the child never has to know."

He was surprised to find that that stung.

Marcus had always wanted to be a father. One day.

He shook his head.

Of course Marcus was worried about Pepper, and he knew that if this midwife was as good as Chase believed, it would be an asset to keep her in St. John. But was this truly the only way?

Aren't you a little too old to take part in a scheme like this?

Marcus shook that thought away, and he couldn't help but wonder what Matthew would think if he knew what was happening. He could only imagine that he would disapprove. Matthew was always the responsible one, but he wasn't sure about that now. Victoria had certainly relaxed his uptight brother.

Maybe he would think this was smart, a straightforward way to help multiple people.

Doubtful. It's fraud.

A quick search on Google told Marcus that he would essentially be tricking the government so that this midwife could stay in the country. If they got caught, she'd be deported and he would be fined, jailed and would probably lose his medical license.

All reasons to say no.

The thing was, he wanted to help Pepper and because he wasn't allowed to return to work for another four weeks, he had time on his hands to at least meet this woman and talk about the possibility. He wasn't planning to ever get married for real, so maybe there was no harm in a convenient marriage for the time being.

Of course, he wouldn't completely know if it would work until he met Alexis. He hoped he liked her so they could pull this off.

You're doing this for Pepper and Chase.

They had always been there for him. Especially in the years after he had came back from California, when his heart was in tatters after Dawna, when his brother wasn't part of his life and his parents were too busy traveling around the world to recognize that their son was hurting.

Chase and Pepper had been his family.

He could do this for his family.

Couldn't he?

Alexis winced.

Great.

She had to use the bathroom.

Again.

Pregnancy was the miracle of life and

Alexis had always envied her patients secretly, but this having to go to the bathroom every few minutes was getting old quickly.

Not that she really minded, of course. For most of her adult life, she'd been told by her own OB/GYN in London that she had unexplained infertility and so the fact that she was pregnant at all was a miracle.

She and her ex-husband had tried everything over the years, desperate to have a child, a family.

At least that's what she'd thought they both wanted.

The moment she finally became pregnant was the exact moment that her husband, Bruce, the man she'd loved for the last five years, told her that he actually didn't want a family. He thought that she would eventually give up trying to get pregnant when all the avenues had failed, and then they could enjoy their life together.

He'd been so angry six months ago when he found out she was pregnant.

And then he'd left her and filed for divorce. His reason? That she deceived him. He claimed he had married her specifically because he believed she couldn't have children, and so the pregnancy voided their agreement.

If that wasn't the complete kicker, he also quickly began a new relationship with someone else.

It was then that Alexis knew that it wasn't the pregnancy that had made him end their marriage. Bruce had moved on from her long before that, and had been making plans to leave. It crushed her completely, but it also gave her the push she needed to close that chapter of her life. There was no point in trying to hold on to something that toxic.

She'd been blinded by love, and she wasn't going to let that happen ever again.

Alexis gladly signed the decree of divorce and made sure that Bruce signed over all claims to their unborn child so that she would have sole custody and parental control once the baby was born. She wasn't going to have him swoop in later and try to disrupt her child's life. She'd had a father like that— an absentee father who cared more about his work than his family—and she wouldn't put her own child through that.

She'd seen the toll it had taken on her mother.

It was still a burden on her to this day.

There were times when Alexis had wanted to tell her mother to run, but she knew her mother would never listen to her. So instead of having her baby go through that, Alexis sold her flat in London for a tidy sum, quit her practice and headed to the US Virgin Islands on a short-term contract.

An escape to paradise had sounded like the perfect next step.

The problem was that now that her four-month work visa was up, she found that she didn't want to leave St. John. She was in love with the island, the people and all of her patients.

Alexis had never felt more at home than she did here.

This was where she wanted to raise her child.

The problem was, she couldn't stay.

It was breaking her heart. As if in response to her worried thoughts, there was a tiny kick, almost like a nudge or a poke. Alexis smiled and rubbed the small swell in her lower belly.

"I know you want to stay, too."

"Are you talking to yourself again?"

Alexis looked up from her desk in the clinic to see Chase Fredrick standing in the doorway. Her stomach sank.

"Is it Pepper? Is she having a flare-up?" Alexis asked nervously.

Pepper Fredrick was one of the patients that Alexis didn't want to leave.

The woman had a lot going on—her son had recently had a kidney transplant in a major domino surgery, and she was eight months pregnant and high risk. She had sickle cell anemia, and Alexis had been surprised to find that none of the other midwives she worked with on St. John had dealt with it before. Alexis had seen it many times and Pepper was in her care, but beyond that, Pepper and Chase had been like a surrogate family to her since she'd arrived.

And she didn't want to leave them.

She wanted her baby and Pepper's baby to be best friends.

Alexis had never experienced the support and the community that she got here and couldn't imagine finding it again anywhere else. Even though she had biological family in England, she was mostly alone there.

Plus England reminded her of Bruce and his betrayal. It held too much sadness, too many memories she wanted to leave behind for good.

St. John made her happy and this is where she wanted to stay, but she had to go back to England. She had been so busy with work she'd left things too late. By the time she returned to England and applied for another visa, she'd be too pregnant to travel back safely and she'd be stuck, unable to be here to help Pepper through what would be a tricky final few weeks of her pregnancy.

"No, it's not Pepper. Pepper is fine. I've come here to tell you that I have a solution to your problem!"

Alexis cocked an eyebrow. She was intrigued.

"You have a solution to indigestion and my need to use the bathroom every five minutes?" she teased.

Chase grinned. "No, but wouldn't that solve a lot of problems? I have a solution to your visa problem. I have a way to keep you in the country."

Alexis smiled. A miracle solution at this late stage seemed too good to be true. She'd already spent ages racking her brain, trying to think of something—anything—that would keep her here legally, but she hadn't come up with anything.

"What is it?" she asked, trying not to appear too eager or to get her hopes up.

"Well, it was Pepper's idea actually."

As soon as he said that, Alexis knew exactly what Chase was going to say, because Pepper had already suggested it to her. She had come up with some inventive ideas in the short time she had known her, but her latest had taken the cake. It was straight out of one of those novels that Pepper was devouring regularly.

And that was the problem with it.

It was fiction.

It wasn't real life. People did not have marriage of conveniences. It was too far-fetched.

"No. Absolutely not. I'm not getting married," Alexis said quickly.

That was a hard pass for her. There was no way that she was putting herself through that again. Bruce had hurt her, shattered her trust. She would have to be an absolute raving lunatic to try and attempt another marriage.

Even if it was fake.

"How did you…? Oh. Pepper already told you, didn't she?"

Alexis nodded and stood up. "She did and it's a wild notion. Stuff like that doesn't happen in real life."

"Of course it does," Chase said. "People pretend to be married all the time. This is your only option, Alexis. It's not a real marriage. You just have to pretend for a while so you can stay in the country."

"A green card takes a long time, Chase. You do realize that?" she asked.

Chase nodded. "Of course."

"Who is going to be fake married to me for two-plus years without some kind of compensation? I can't afford that."

"The man in question doesn't want compensation."

"So he's doing it out of the goodness of his heart?" she asked in disbelief.

"Yes." Chase grinned.

"Seems too good to be true."

"Some would say that about him. Not me, mind you. What do you say, Alexis?"

Alexis worried her bottom lip.

She really did want to stay in the country. She wanted to be able to take care of her patients, and she wanted her and her baby to start a new life here.

She'd never really been happy in England, but here in St. John she'd discovered her happy place. She loved everything about this island. The warm breezes, the greenery, the people, the food, the white sand beaches and the turquoise sea.

There were so many mornings where she

would just sit at the window in her small room, staring out over the water and watching the big cruise ships slowly sail by on their way to Charlotte Amalie on St. Thomas.

It made her want to explore even more, to see all the different corners of St. Croix and then maybe even leave the US Virgin Islands and head out to other countries like Jamaica, Haiti, or Cuba. Maybe even farther south.

She always had a secret dream of getting a boat and sailing around the world.

Bruce hadn't been into that idea.

She should've taken it as a warning sign, but she'd been young and in love.

Alexis shook her head, clearing her dreams out of her mind so that she could focus on what Chase was saying.

"If I do decide to attempt this idea of Pepper's, who is going to agree to marry me?"

Chase grinned, his brown eyes twinkling. "I have just the man for you. A stand-up citizen and native son to the islands. Alexis Martin, may I introduce you to your future husband and my best friend, Dr. Marcus Olesen."

Alexis's eyes widened when she realized Chase had brought the man with him, and the moment that this Marcus Olesen walked into her office her breath was nearly taken away. Her pulse quickened as she gazed into the bluest eyes she'd ever seen. He had sandy blond hair that was a little longer than she usually liked, but somehow it suited him. He had a neatly trimmed beard, and the way his eyes twinkled at her made her knees shake.

A little voice inside Alexis told her that this man was a bit of a rogue—that he could be dangerous to her heart—and she was annoyed the way her body responded to him.

The way he took her breath away.

It took her a minute to find her voice as she was forced to swallow the lump that had suddenly formed in her throat.

"It's a pleasure to meet you," she finally squeaked out.

He smiled, but that smile didn't extend to his eyes, which made her suspect that he wasn't exactly a willing participant in this either.

"Pleasure," he said stiffly. His gaze roved over her body in a way that made her blood heat and yet made her feel vulnerable.

Naked.

Exposed.

This man was a definite danger. He was a temptation.

Chase was still smiling, obviously proud of himself and confident that this had worked out and was already a done deal. "I'm going to figure out what we have to do next about the marriage, so I'll leave you two to get acquainted."

Alexis didn't want to be alone to Marcus. Not that she didn't trust him, but because he was making her feel things she hadn't felt in a long time and she didn't ever want to feel this way again. She was almost annoyed with herself for having had such a strong initial reaction to him.

"So…" she said once they were alone, her voice shaking ever so slightly.

Marcus shoved his hands in the pockets of his khaki-colored Bermuda shorts. "So, when are we going to get on with this sham?"

CHAPTER TWO

THE MOMENT HE said the words, he instantly regretted them.

He had been standing in the hall and listening to her and Chase. Marcus knew that Alexis wasn't really keen on this either, but she was doing this for Pepper and he could appreciate that. What he hadn't expected was how stunningly beautiful she was.

She was glowing.

Marcus couldn't remember the last time that he had actually had his breath taken away by a woman.

Actually he could. The last time was Dawna.

He shook that niggling thought away. Since Dawna, he'd been out on countless dates, but there had been very few second dates and definitely no long-term commitments.

It was one of the reasons he preferred to date tourists—because there was always an end date. Their time together was short, sweet and he didn't have to ever contemplate committing to just one woman.

Marcus didn't have to put his heart at risk.

It was so much better that way.

Is it?

He shoved that thought to the back of his mind.

It really didn't matter. He was here to marry Alexis so she could continue to take care of Pepper and all the other pregnant women in her care. He didn't need to get attached. The fact he was so attracted to her was a bit unnerving, but nothing he couldn't handle.

Her golden hair fell in soft waves around her heart-shaped face. Dark brown eyes, intense like a storm, met his gaze, and there was a slight peachy tinge to her creamy cheeks. He towered over her, but then that wasn't a surprise given he was over six feet.

The only woman who towered over him was Matthew's wife, Victoria, and that's because she insisted on wearing crazy tall heels.

Alexis might like those same kinds of heels, but she was wearing ballet flats at present, likely because of her pregnancy. His gazed roved over her body and settled on the swell of her abdomen. He'd guess she was about six months along, if this was her first, as it took longer to show in a first pregnancy.

A marriage of convenience meant it was going to be hard to keep his distance from her, but he would have to get control of himself because he currently couldn't tear his gaze from her. To try and shake himself out of his daze, he'd resorted to surliness.

And he regretted that.

This whole situation wasn't Alexis's fault. It wasn't her idea.

"I'm sorry I sounded rude just now. I guess I'm still in shock."

She smiled, looking relieved. "I am too. Shocked, I mean."

"I mean, it's a ruse after all."

"Yes," she said in her plummy British accent. "I suppose it is a sham, isn't it?"

"Yes, but I told Chase that I would help. Pepper and the new baby are the priority now."

"You do realize this is possibly a two-year commitment? It says on every piece of information about this process that it can take eighteen to twenty-four months to be approved. It's a lot to ask… Sorry, I didn't quite catch your name."

"Marcus. Dr. Marcus Olesen."

Her brow furrowed, and she cocked her head to one side. "Wait, you're Dr. Olesen? Are you the surgeon that completed that domino surgery a few weeks ago?"

"No. That was my brother. I was involved though."

"So you're a surgeon?"

"No," he said quickly.

He never wanted to be mistaken for a surgeon. It was bad enough his brother had always pressured him to be a surgeon, and that his parents always kept going on about him being more like Matthew, but it was Dawna's leaving him for a surgeon that was the gut punch he couldn't handle and still couldn't quite move past.

Being a surgeon didn't always mean that you were better. He loved being a general practitioner. He did miss the fast pace of the emergency room from California, but he loved his practice here too. He formed relationships with his patients, he got to know them and he saw them for more than just a preoperative and postoperative visit.

It was more than cutting them open and patching them back up again.

You know that's not what Matthew does.

He felt bad for thinking it.

A pink tinge colored her cheeks. "I'm sorry, I assumed when you said that you were involved in the domino… Well, I thought you were a surgeon."

"I was involved because I was a donor. Chase and Pepper's son, Jonas, is my godson and I did it for him."

"So you donated your kidney to him?" she asked.

"No, not exactly. I donated my kidney to a patient who was a difficult match and her donor donated to Jonas. That's how the domino works. You have donors and recipients who are all mismatched but everyone ends up getting what they need. It was complicated, and I know there was a lot of paperwork and charts to keep it all straight. I was part of it, and even I don't feel like I can explain it well enough to people."

She quirked her eyebrow, her eyes widening. "That's a massive undertaking, but I understand the basics. Surgery is not my cup of tea. I could handle it, but just didn't like dealing with unconscious patients and surgeons all the time. Plus the smell and feel of an operating room has always bothered me."

He softened to her last remark because he

felt the same way too. "It's the cautery and the cold I don't like."

"Quite." She smiled again, tucking a strand of blond hair behind her ear. "Still, a domino is quite fascinating all the same."

"It was, but I'm not here to talk about the domino. I'm here to talk to you about this marriage of convenience."

Alexis blushed again and sat down. She motioned for him to sit in the chair opposite, which he did gladly. He was thankful for the seat so he could rest. His side was bothering him and that was annoying. It frustrated him how long it was taking to heal.

"I want to thank you for doing this," she said quickly. "It seems to me that you've given so much to Chase and Pepper already."

"It's my pleasure."

He wasn't being entirely truthful. He was glad to be helping out his friends, but there was a part of him that was telling him that this wasn't the right thing to do. Especially now, having met Alexis. There was a part of him telling him that this was a bad idea and that he should run in the opposite direction, that his heart was in danger of being hurt.

Badly.

"We both know this is a long commitment and one between strangers," she said.

"Agreed."

"So, where do we even begin?"

"At the start." He smiled and she smiled back.

"Right. First things first. I think we'll have to start to get to know one another. Learn some basic information about each other, but I promise you that it will only be basic. I'm not completely comfortable with this situation or having a stranger know too much about my personal life."

Her honesty shocked him, but she wasn't wrong. They were strangers, and it would be prudent for him not to get too close to her. They would do what was necessary to convince the world their marriage was true and then, once Alexis got a green card, they would get a divorce. And if no one bothered with them in the meantime, they could live separate lives. He wouldn't have to get too involved in her life or the life of her child.

Her pregnancy was the major cause of his hesitation with this plan. There was a child involved, and he wouldn't do anything to hurt an innocent life.

As much as Marcus had always dreamed

about having a wife and kids, when Dawna left him he had laid those dreams to rest. They weren't meant to be.

Matthew didn't think he would get married again, but he did.

Marcus ignored that voice and was annoyed that his conscience was becoming that little bit more vocal lately. It was unwelcome.

This marriage of convenience with Alexis was a business arrangement and nothing more.

And he had to keep reminding himself of that.

Alexis was having a hard time focusing. She had a vague idea of the basic information that Immigration would need, or ask, if they were questioned about their quickie marriage, but for some strange reason she just couldn't focus on it.

Not only was Marcus devilishly handsome, but he was also a kind soul. He was a bit of a hero stepping up and giving a kidney to a stranger in a complicated procedure just so his godson could get a kidney in return.

It was the gift of life, and it was priceless.

His lips were pursed in a thin line, and she couldn't help but wonder if he was in pain.

She knew from Pepper that Jonas's surgery had been two months ago now, but he was obviously having some postoperative pain, and she felt bad that he had been dragged here, in the heat, to help her.

Alexis wasn't sure how or when she would ever be able to pay him back for the favor he was offering to do for her. She would be indebted to him.

"Maybe we should do this another day?" she said gently.

"What do you mean?" he asked stiffly.

"The getting-to-know-you questions. Maybe today is not the day."

"Today seems like a good enough time. Besides, knowing Chase, he'll pack us off to the courthouse in Charlotte Amalie to get married in an hour."

Alexis chuckled. "You're right. He's quite tenacious."

"Exactly. Why do you want to put it off?"

"You seem to be quite uncomfortable. And I mean pain wise. It's from the surgery, isn't it?"

"It is and I am, but I'm okay. The only way that I'm going to be able to return to my practice is if I push myself a bit more each day."

"I'm no surgeon, but I am a trained nurse

practitioner in addition to being a midwife, and you have to rest," she said, as gently as she could.

Marcus had opened his mouth to say something further when one of the administrative staff who worked near the entrance of the clinic rushed into the room.

"Alexis!"

She jumped up, as fast as her pregnant belly allowed her to. "What's wrong, Margaret?"

The woman took a deep breath. "It's Mrs. Winston. She's on the floor of the waiting room, in labor. Her water broke and there's a lot of blood in it. We can't get her to Charlotte Amalie on a ferry, but an air ambulance has been called. Her husband is overseas and her mother is watching the other kids. She's alone."

Alexis swallowed the lump in her throat. "I'm coming."

"Can I help?" Marcus asked.

"Yes. Most of the midwife staff has left for the day. I'll need all the help I can get!"

Marcus nodded and followed Alexis out of her office. It was just a short distance to the waiting room. Alexis could tell that Mrs. Winston was in far more pain than she should be, and with the amount of brightly colored blood in the fluid on the floor, the first thing Alexis suspected was a placental abruption.

She'd seen this before.

Most of the time, it would mean the mother-to-be would need a Cesarean section, but that was beyond her abilities, and as they weren't set up for a surgery here, it wasn't an option.

"You said you called for the air ambulance from Charlotte Amalie?" Alexis said to Margaret.

"Yes, I already called Ziese Memorial and they're sending one."

Alexis grabbed one of the ready sterile birthing kits and carefully knelt beside Mrs. Winston.

"Marcie, tell me what happened. You were only four centimeters dilated when you had your appointment." Alexis spoke softly, trying not to alarm or panic her patient.

Marcie Winston panted. "I don't know. I was feeling fine—this is my fourth and I was planning on sticking around nearby so I'd be ready when the baby comes—but then it felt like I was hit in the stomach. It hurts so bad."

"I know. I'm so sorry." Alexis felt Marcie's belly. It was hard as a contraction moved through it, but there were strong kicks. "I'm going to do an exam. Is that okay?"

Marcie nodded Alexis draped her and then removed Marcie's undergarments.

She'd seen this before, when she had done training in Kenya, where hospitals were also few and far between.

Alexis would prefer to have her patient safely in hospital, but the baby was coming, and until the air ambulance came Alexis was all Marcie had.

"I'm just going to check to see how dilated you are." Alexis asked, gaining consent. She never took that it was implied. She wanted all her patients to be comfortable.

"Yes. Please. Just help," Marcie begged.

Alexis nodded and her did her exam. Marcie's four centimeters had turned into ten and she was now fully effaced. Alexis could see the baby making its way. This baby was coming fast and furious.

At this point there was no waiting for the helicopter.

"What can I do?" Marcus asked.

"Can you sit behind her, hold her? This baby is coming." Alexis readied what she needed. The rest of the staff in the clinic knew what to do as Marcus took his place be-hind Marcie, to help brace her as she pushed. Marcie was so weak Alexis was glad Marcus was here to help her.

"What's happening?" Mrs. Winston, asked.

"Marcie, your baby is coming. Fast. I think your placenta has detached, so we need to get the baby out as fast as we can. I know it hurts, but you're going to have to push," Alexis said encouragingly. She knew that it was going to be painful for Marcie, even though this wasn't her first baby. The placenta was tearing and the baby wasn't stopping.

"You can do this," Marcus said gently from behind Marcie, holding her shoulders as she bore down and pushed.

"You're doing so great," Alexis told her. She kept one hand on Marcie's abdomen as she kept her focus on the beautiful life that was being born into the world. This was why she loved her work so much.

Watching life begin.

The miracle of birth.

And soon it would be her, in another mid-wife's hands, as she brought forth her little miracle. She just wished that she had someone to share it with. She had thought Bruce was going to be that person.

Don't think about it now.

With a couple more pushes, Marcie's baby girl was born. Alexis cleared the baby's mouth and soon there was a lusty cry, angry at being ejected from a warm and safe place into a cold, bright world.

Marcie cried and held out her arms for the baby.

Usually Alexis liked to keep the baby attached to the cord until the placenta was delivered, but it wasn't possible in this instance, so she clamped and cut the cord. Margaret handed her a blanket and they wrapped the little girl before handing her over to her mother.

That's when the bleeding started, and Alexis knew for certain that it was an abruption.

"Do you have a Foley catheter?" Marcus asked.

"We do." Alexis stood and got one.

"Insert it and pack it. We don't want it to tear away from the uterine wall. I would suggest a massage on her abdomen, but if the placenta has abrupted she'll need surgery."

Alexis nodded as Marcus came to sit beside her, pulling on gloves. He got sterile sponges and dressings, helping her as they packed Marcie to try and staunch the flow.

"Marcie, how are you doing?" Marcus asked.

"Not. Good. Tired," Marcie said, her words slurred.

Marcus took the baby. "Try and relax, the helicopter is nearly here."

"Okay," Marcie murmured.

In the background Alexis could hear the whir of the helicopter blades making an emergency landing out in the parking lot, and not a moment too soon.

There was so much blood.

Alexis watched Marcus hold the little girl so gently. He was so calm.

She was impressed that a general practitioner knew what to do in the case of a placental abruption. Usually only a midwife, nurse or obstetrician dealt with this situation enough to know what to do.

"What's her blood pressure?" Alexis grimly asked Margaret, who was monitoring it.

"It's eighty-nine over fifty-five," Margaret responded.

Alexis pursed her lips as the paramedics from Ziese Memorial Hospital came rushing into the clinic with a stretcher. Alexis stood up and took off her gloves as she started to fill them in on what had happened so far.

"This mother—gravida four, para four—has just delivered a female infant. There was quite a lot of blood and pain. I suspect a placental abruption. Her blood pressure is eight-nine systolic over fifty-five diastolic. She has not delivered the placenta yet. We placed a Foley catheter and packed her to try and staunch the bleeding."

The head paramedic nodded. "We'll take her to her OB/GYN surgeon who is ready and waiting."

"Please keep me posted on her progress."

The paramedic nodded, and Alexis stepped back as the paramedics got Mrs. Winston stable on the stretcher. There wasn't any room on the air ambulance for them, but Alexis was familiar with Dr. Baxter at Ziese Memorial Hospital and she was comfortable leaving Marcie in Dr. Baxter's capable hands.

Marcus made sure the baby was settled with her mother and was helping the paramedic hooking up the intravenous to get Marcie fluids.

She and Margaret sent Marcie's file electronically to the head of obstetrics at Ziese

Memorial, and then there was nothing more Alexis could do.

"You did a great job," Marcus said.

"I'm not the only one," Alexis stated. "I was impressed by how you stepped in like that."

Marcus cocked an eyebrow. "Oh, really?"

"Yes. You knew right away to use a Foley catheter and about the massage."

"Well, I've had to deal with an unexpected birth or two in my time." He winced as he walked over to where she was standing, and she felt bad.

"Are you okay?" she asked.

"Just my incision site. It's taking me a bit longer to heal than I'd like and reminding me that I'm not as young as I once was." He half smiled, and there was a twinkle in his blue eyes.

Alexis couldn't help but smile back.

He was charming. She'd give him that.

They just stood there in awkward silence.

"Why don't we go talk in private?" Alexis finally offered.

Marcus nodded and they walked back to her office.

"So, like I was saying before, I suppose

we need to get to know one another, make some appearances together to firm this whole thing up," Marcus said as he shut the door to her office.

"Yes. I suppose. I have to admit though that I'm apprehensive about this. I'm not quite sure it'll work."

"It apparently does, or people wouldn't even attempt it. I won't lie. I'm nervous about this, too, but we have to give it a try. How about we have dinner tonight? Say, around eight? We can go somewhere private and hash this thing all out. I'll cook."

"That sounds good," she replied.

It would be nice to get out of her little room at the dormitory.

She'd been here four months and hadn't really seen much of the island. She'd been too busy working and trying to get over her broken heart. Or rather, trying to get over her anger at being betrayed by the man who had promised to be by her side forever, in sickness and in health.

St. John was her fresh start and she wanted to stay.

This was going to be the start of her new life, and she'd do whatever it took to make it happen. Even fake a marriage to a charming man who was sacrificing his freedom—his life for the next two years—for her.

A stranger.

CHAPTER THREE

MARCUS KNEW THE moment the words came out of his mouth that it was a mistake to invite Alexis for dinner. Usually, when he asked a woman out on a dinner date, it was an opportunity to charm and seduce her.

Dates were casual.

Fun.

But the women he usually went out with were in and out of his life quickly. Anything they shared was always temporary.

Alexis would be in his life for a long while.

Yes, the marriage would just be on paper—they wouldn't really have a relationship—but he couldn't be caught dating around for the next couple of years, or the truth of their sham marriage would be exposed.

There was a part of him that wanted more with Alexis, maybe even a real relationship, but he quickly silenced that part and reminded himself that she was off-limits. This whole situation with Alexis was just a business arrangement. He wasn't here for romance. His heart wasn't open to that.

This was a marriage of convenience so that a talented midwife and nurse practitioner could stay in the country and take care of Pepper.

And there was no doubt in his mind that Alexis was talented. He'd seen her in action himself.

If the midwife clinic hadn't been there, if Mrs. Winston had gone into labor on her own at home, she would've bled out and died.

It was imperative that Alexis was able to stay and continue to provide this kind of service to the island of St. John. There was also part of him that acknowledged he could learn from her, so that he could better take care of his patients. As a general practitioner and with midwives on the islands, as well as a state-of-the-art hospital in Charlotte Amalie, there wasn't much call for him to attend births. But he found he wanted to learn—and he wanted Alexis to be the one to teach him.

He may not have always taken school as seriously as Matthew told him he should, but Marcus liked to learn and he liked to better himself...

* * *

"You could be a surgeon," Dawna said.

Marcus looked up from his charting. "Why? I like being a general practitioner. I get to develop real relationships with my patients."

Dawna rolled her eyes. "That's not where the money is though."

"I don't care about that. Money isn't everything."

"You're so hopeless," she said with a sigh.

Marcus shook that thought away. At the time he thought Dawna was teasing him, but now he realized they'd never quite seen eye to eye on the monetary issue. For Dawna, in the end, it was a big deal.

"So what are we having for dinner?" Alexis asked. "Is there anything you want me to bring?"

The question caught him off guard. He hadn't really thought much beyond inviting her. He would usually have dinner catered, but there wasn't much time to organize that at this point in the day.

"I don't know. You could bring dessert?"

Alexis nodded. "I can."

"Okay."

"You still didn't answer my question though. What're we having?"

"Are there foods that bother you?" he asked gently. "Or are you just picky?"

She grinned. "Not picky, but some things do inflame my morning sickness, and there are some things I just can't eat right now."

Marcus leaned back against her desk. "Like what?"

"Tomatoes," she stated. "Used to love them and I can't stand them now—not even sauces or ketchups or catsups or anything tomato adjacent."

"That's a shame. So no to tomatoes…"

"Or fish, or sushi or… I'm being a pest now, aren't I?"

"No." He smiled at her. "You're not. I think I can whip up something you'd like."

"I look forward to it."

Marcus got up. "Well, I'd better get ready. Shall I pick you up at the dorm?"

"That sounds wonderful."

Marcus left with an unexpected spring in his step. He was actually looking forward to dinner tonight. He always liked the dates he made, but this was something different and he couldn't quite put his finger on it.

Alexis was so different from the women

he felt were a safe bet. Women he wouldn't get attached to.

He smiled to himself as he thought of how she had gone right to work when alerted to her patient's emergency and how focused she'd been throughout the surprise delivery. She didn't shy away from the challenge. Instead, she was gentle and kind, in total control as she took command.

And she was intelligent.

All qualities that he liked in a woman.

His pulse quickened as he thought of her, and all his old instincts kicked in. Matthew had always accused him of being a ladies' man, a notion that Marcus scoffed at, but maybe he was right. He'd always enjoyed the company of women but only when he had the safety net of his companions' firm departure date. It was different with Alexis though. He couldn't get her out of his mind.

He was thinking of her silken blond hair, her dark brown eyes and the peachy pink tinge to her cheeks that had appeared when he'd caused her to blush.

She's pregnant, you dolt.

And that was the kicker. She was six months pregnant with another man's child. Marcus didn't know what kind of relationship, if any, she currently had with the baby's father. Maybe once she got her green card she'd go back to him.

Alexis was not his.

And wouldn't be.

So he had to keep telling himself that this marriage of convenience was just that.

A contract.

A piece of paper.

Nothing more.

In a short amount of time he would be divorced. Or rather, *they* would be divorced and then he could get on with his life.

What life?

That was the crux of the matter. He didn't really have a life. At least not the one he'd always pictured. By now, according the original plans he'd made when he fell for Dawna, he should have a couple of kids of his own.

A house.

A wife.

Heck, he could even have a kid the same age as his godson, who was fifteen.

And then it struck him just how long ago he had made those plans for himself. What had he been doing with his life in the meantime?

Not living it, a little voice inside him whispered.

Marcus picked up supplies for salad, garlic bread and fettuccine Alfredo on the way home. He'd made it often before, usually for his late sister-in-law, Kirsten, because it was her favorite, but this was the first time he was cooking it for someone else, someone outside his family.

Having showered, changed and prepped everything for dinner, Marcus finally glanced at the clock and realized that he was late picking up Alexis. He cursed under his breath and disembarked his boat, the *Tryphine*, which was named for the patron saint of pregnant mothers, overdue mothers and sick children.

He ran down the gangplank and hopped into his small car, which was a beat-up thing that he drove around the island of St. John. Mostly, he preferred to get around by boat, but Marcus still hadn't been cleared for heavy lifting, so he couldn't exactly sail his boat on his own.

It was a short drive to the dormitories were the locum midwives were posted, and he found Alexis waiting outside for him. For the second time that day, she nearly took his breath away. She was wearing a long, flowery dress that was blowing in the breeze, and her blond hair fell in waves down over her bared shoulders.

She reminded him a bit of the painting of Venus in the clamshell, and his heart skipped a beat.

Marcus parked the car and got out to open the door for her. She blushed when he did that, tucking an errant strand of hair behind her ear, and he caught a whiff of green tea and honey as she moved. He wanted to lean forward and breathe that intoxicating scent in deeper, but knew he had to stop himself.

"Thank you," she said, her voice shaking slightly.

"You're welcome." He shut the door and ran back to the driver's side and climbed in.

"So where are we going?" she asked.

"You're full of questions."

"I ask questions when I'm nervous," she admitted.

"Are you nervous?" he asked.

"A bit. I don't know you."

"I don't bite. Much." He grinned and she laughed.

"Okay. Fine. So we're going to a mystery spot."

"No mystery. I told you I'd cook for you so we're going to my place. I live at the marina, in case you want to let someone know where you are."

She smiled appreciatively. "Thanks. I mean, we're technically strangers. I know you're Chase and Pepper's friend, but I still don't know *you*. I have to protect myself. And you told me you do bite, albeit not much."

Marcus laughed. "Fair enough. And you're right. We're strangers. If we're going to pull off this marriage, then we have to get to know one another better in case someone asks us questions about how we met or our 'relationship.'"

Alexis smiled and nodded. "Thank you. I'm glad you see it my way."

"You've been thanking me a lot, and I haven't even really laid on the charm." He grinned and winked. She laughed softly.

"Is that supposed to be some kind of pickup line?"

"No, just the truth."

"My, my…aren't we full of ourself?"

He glanced over at her and was relieved to see she was smiling. She was teasing him, and he couldn't help but laugh. He was glad she was someone who could take a joke, and that she was someone whom he could tease.

It would make their marriage seem more

real, because it would appear to be so much more natural if they had a good rapport. As much as he wanted to stay a stranger to her, to keep away because he was so drawn to her, that wouldn't be good for their ruse.

"I'm sorry, I don't usually tease a stranger in such a familiar way," she apologized.

"No. I like it. I tease my brother something fierce now."

One of her finely arched brows quirked. "Now? That seems to imply that the relationship wasn't always so strong."

"It wasn't," Marcus admitted. Which was the truth. There had been a point growing up when Matthew had taken it upon himself to almost parent him, and Marcus had resented his brother for it. He wanted a brother, not a warden, but Matthew was so serious, so worried.

The thing that frustrated Marcus the most was that there had been no reason for Matthew to have taken on that role. They had two parents—why couldn't they just have been brothers, there for one another?

"I'm sorry to hear that," she said.

"We're doing better now. Since my kidney donation, we've grown closer. It's a bit tenuous still, but it's a lot better than it was and

I credit his wife, Vic, with a lot of my brother's softening."

Alexis smiled. "I hope I get to meet them."

"I'm sure you will." Marcus worried what Matthew would think about this whole situation. Would Matthew's parenting instinct kick in, setting them back? He could almost hear Matthew's voice now berating him for agreeing to such a foolish venture as a marriage of convenience. "Do you have any siblings?" he asked, trying to change the subject.

"No. I'm an only child."

She didn't elaborate. Just pressed her lips together in a firm line as if she was done talking about it. He'd seen patients do that before, unwilling to give up information, even if they knew that it would affect their health and that Marcus needed to know.

He wasn't going to press her about it right now, but he needed to know about her family eventually if he was going to pose as her husband. He parked his car in his parking space outside the marina and turned off the ignition, climbing out and opening her door again. She seemed confused as she looked around.

"You live down here?" she asked.

"Yes. On a boat."

"A boat?" she asked, surprised.

"Well, I did say I live at the marina. What did you expect?"

"I honestly don't know. I've never met a person who lived on a boat before."

"It's how I travel around the islands and visit my patients. When I'm practicing, that is. Right now, I haven't been cleared by my surgeon to go back to work just yet."

"I would've never pictured you as a boat type of person," she said.

He cocked his head to one side. "And what kind of person is a boat type of person?"

Alexis laughed nervously. "I don't know. I guess maybe someone with more stripes on their clothing—more navy and white. And they'd probably always wear deck shoes. Maybe even a nice white hat?"

"Well, at least you're picturing me as the skipper rather than a pirate," he teased.

She laughed. "Well, if your beard was a bit more scraggly, then maybe… Yeah, you'd look very pirate-like. Or maybe if you had a gold earring?"

"Thanks for the suggestions, but I think I'll just remain the inconspicuous boat person that you know me as."

The sun was setting, and all the lights

strung on other masts made the marina look like a magical place, rather than just a bunch of boats moored together.

He stopped in front of the *Tryphine*.

"This is beautiful," she said in awe.

Marcus smiled.

Even with the sails down it *was* beautiful. Made of polished wood, the boat had a navy blue hull.

"Thanks. It was custom-built for my father in the late seventies, when it was super-chic to have a yacht like this. It was built by a naval architect who designed yachts that were meant for world travel and racing, though my father didn't do either."

"So why have a sailboat like this?"

Marcus grinned. "My father likes to have the best, but he doesn't have sea legs, or rather, doesn't have the sea legs to man a sailboat. There were a lot of unexpected swims in the sea and a mishap with a shark, so he gave me the sailboat. He has a motorized yacht now."

He instinctively held out his hand to help her aboard, and as she slipped her tiny, delicate hand into his he felt a jolt of electricity, a zing, pass through him.

It caught him by surprise.

As did the fact that he didn't want to let go.

"I hope there isn't retro seventies decor inside, like shag carpet and big gold and brown flowers," she said teasingly.

"And if there were?"

"Are there?" she asked, surprised.

"No, there was, but I retrofitted the inside myself to something more classic and sleek."

Marcus helped her down into his home. The *Tryphine* was his baby. His passion since he'd come back from California and his father gave it to him.

His brother got the luxury car and Marcus got the boat. It was in more disrepair than his brother's car, because it had sat dry-docked in Miami for some time, but Marcus hadn't cared. He'd wanted—needed—to do something to get his mind off what Dawna had done to his heart.

Kirsten, Matthew's late wife, had also encouraged him to pursue the renovations.

In fact, she was the one who had been responsible for picking out the colors, and he liked that there was a bit of his dearly beloved late sister-in-law here.

The name she'd given the boat was her real legacy though…

* * *

"What shall I call it? I really don't want a boat named after my mother," Marcus stated. He planned to seduce women on this boat and having a boat named after your mom was not conducive to that...

Matthew rolled his eyes. *"There's nothing wrong with* Freja.*"*

Kirsten scolded him. *"Don't be so mean to your brother. He's absolutely right that this is his vessel now, and he needs to choose a name he likes."*

"Don't you like my mother?" Matthew teased.

Marcus couldn't help but be envious of them and the love they shared in that intimate, teasing moment.

"You know that I do," Kirsten said sweetly. *"Still, a single man shouldn't have a boat named after this mother."*

Marcus stuck his tongue out at Matthew and then laughed. He was glad that Kirsten was siding with him.

"Don't be childish, Marcus," Matthew groused, trying not to laugh as well.

"Don't be such a stick in the mud, Matthew," Marcus snapped back. *"Kirsten, since*

you're always kind and sweet to me I want you to name her."

Kirsten smiled. "How about Tryphine*?"*

"What?" Matthew asked, confused.

"The patron saint of sick children, I believe," Marcus said.

"And of overdue mothers," Kirsten said sadly. "Mothers who never got to be mothers..."

The brothers shared a look. Marcus knew too how much Kirsten wanted a child. And with the cancer that just wasn't possible at the moment. If anyone deserved to be a mother, it was her and Marcus hurt for her more than ever in that moment.

"Tryphine it is, then!" Marcus announced. "She'll be the only one in the Caribbean, I'm sure."

He smiled at the memory.

"Are you okay?" Alexis asked, interrupting his thoughts.

"Yes. Fine, just thinking about something. Why don't you have a seat, and I'll get you a glass of lemonade?"

She smiled. "That would be great."

Marcus headed into the galley as Alexis made herself comfortable at the table that sat under the windows at stern. He closed the small pocket door that led into the galley, trying to collect his thoughts.

He was enjoying himself with her.

Too much.

This was going to be a long, trying night.

Alexis couldn't believe that Marcus had a sailboat and that he lived in it full time. One, he said, that was capable of going around the world. That had always been her dream. To sail off into the sunset and discover new places.

She'd wanted to travel so much more when she was younger, but her mother had dissuaded her, always telling her that she'd get murdered or taken advantage of by someone looking for a green card.

Alexis laughed at that thought, because now she was the one taking advantage of Marcus.

Either way, she'd been a little bit more timid back then and had listened to her mother. Then she'd met Bruce and her mother was happy for her. Alexis had thought she was happy too, so she'd let go of all those secret dreams of traveling. She was in love, and Bruce didn't want to live somewhere else. He wanted to stay in England and said she was foolish to want to move to somewhere exotic and start up a life with no family around.

When they'd tried and failed to get pregnant, Bruce had said it was meant to be, that they should just be happy with what they had, even though it broke Alexis's heart that she would never be a mother.

When she did finally become pregnant, and Bruce left her, her mother had actually questioned her about keeping her baby, suggesting that she would never be able to find another husband as a single mother because what man would want to raise another man's baby?

Knowing she was carrying a fragile life inside her, Alexis finally admitted to herself that her mother was controlling and her father was absent. That wasn't any kind of family to lean on or rely on.

It was all the impetus that Alexis needed to leave the toxic life she had been in for far too long. She didn't want to raise her baby in such an environment, so she took the first job she could, as far away as she could.

She wasn't sailing around the world and soon she'd have a baby, but St. John, in the US Virgin Islands, was her paradise.

"One lemonade for the lady."

She looked up to see Marcus come out of

the galley with two tall glasses of lemonade, and her heart literally skipped a beat. It had been a long time since someone had made her swoon like this, and she wasn't even completely sure that Bruce had ever made her feel exactly this way.

Marcus was not what she'd expected, and as she thought about it, she realized she wasn't exactly sure what she had been expecting. She was glad that he different though. It was nice to laugh with someone. It was nice to have a casual conversation again.

She'd been so focused on work, her patients and putting her past behind her that it had been a long time since she'd had a non-work-related conversation with someone. Of course, this meeting was work related in a way, about convincing Immigration that they were a real couple. The thought made her uncomfortable. Alexis was very much aware of what they were doing and that it was illegal, but what other choice did she have?

And if it wasn't for the situation she was in, she likely wouldn't have met Marcus at all, a thought that made her sad, she realized.

Marcus sat down across from her and stared out the aft windows at the marina. "If you squint hard, it could be Paris."

"Why would I want that? This is paradise. It's warm and sunny."

"Not right now. There's a wee chill tonight."

"Not the same chill I'm used to."

He grinned. "I suppose not."

"So," she said, setting the glass on the table. "What do we need to discuss?"

"Everything," Marcus said. "Which seems like a daunting task."

"I'm not sure that we need to know everything." And she didn't want him to know completely everything. After what Bruce did to her heart, she didn't want to be that open and vulnerable with someone. It wasn't safe. "This is a marriage on paper only."

"Right." Marcus nodded, and she got the sense that maybe there were things that he didn't want her to know either.

"So, you have one brother?"

He nodded. "Yes. Dr. Matthew Olesen, chief of surgery at Ziese Memorial Hospital in Charlotte Amalie, St. Thomas."

"Are you from Charlotte Amalie?" she asked.

"No, I was born in St. Croix. My parents are Dutch and American. My father is from the Netherlands and my mother is of Dutch descent, but born and raised in New York. Her family came over on one of the ships fleeing Europe in the 1600s. They were Huguenots, and they settled the area of New Paltz—Sleepy Hollow and all that."

"Doesn't the headless horseman come from there?" Alexis asked, intrigued.

"Yes. Washington Irving did write a story about that, didn't he? Yes, it was set there, and a lot of my mother's ancestors are buried there. You seem to have a fascination with the horseman. Your eyes lit up when you mentioned him."

Alexis felt her cheeks heat. "Well, when I was a child and home alone, I would watch a lot of those cartoons from America and in the autumn they would have all these creepy stories about ghosts and witches. And the horseman. That story fascinated me. I don't know why. I couldn't help but wonder what happened to Ichabod."

Marcus smiled. "Well then, there is something unique I now know about you—you're fascinated with the macabre and Halloween."

She laughed. "I suppose."

"And you? You said you're an only child?"

Alexis nodded. "I am. I was born in London. My parents lived in the north end. They are quite well off, and I was sent to the finest schools but disappointed my father greatly when all I became was a midwife and a nurse practitioner."

"Only?" Marcus asked dryly. "That's something to be quite proud of I think."

"I think so, too," she said softly.

Marcus smiled again, his eyes sparkling in the shadows, and she could feel herself swoon again. They were strangers and yet… this moment with him felt so intimate. Like she'd known him for quite some time already.

"What about the father of your baby?" Marcus asked, breaking the spell and the silence.

Alexis swallowed the lump in her throat. She knew that he was going to ask that question, and she knew that he had to ask that question, but it was still a hard pill to swallow. She didn't like to talk about it because it brought up too many painful memories, too much hurt and betrayal, but then again, it also brought her a sense of unending happiness, because this baby was what she'd always wanted.

"The father is my ex-husband. He told me he always wanted children, and though we tried for a long time, it didn't happen. When we'd finally given up, I became pregnant. I thought he would be happy about it, but he'd changed his mind. It was then I discovered that he'd also changed his mind about me. He'd moved on and started an affair a year before."

"I'm sorry."

Alexis shrugged. "It's fine. It happens all the time."

"It does. Too often. My fiancée left me for another man, so trust me when I say I understand." Marcus reached across the table and took her hand in his. The simple touch sent a warming zing through her. She trembled and pulled her hand out of his, unbalanced by his touch.

He pulled his hand back. "Sorry, I didn't ask if you'd be comfortable with that."

"No," she said. "It just caught me off guard. I mean, we're still almost strangers."

"I'm hoping we'll become friends."

Her heart skipped a beat. "I would like that, too."

Marcus leaned back. "So, will I have to deal with your ex-husband during this?"

"No, Bruce signed away all parental rights. He's back in England and has moved on."

Marcus's eyes widened, as if he was shocked

by that. "Okay. Well, I think we should have something to eat before we continue. This is getting a bit too heavy."

"Food would be divine." She was suddenly very hungry.

"I'll be back in a moment. I didn't make fish or anything like that. I know there are things you shouldn't eat being pregnant."

"I know. I miss sushi completely," Alexis complained.

Marcus grinned. "Just relax and I'll be back in a moment. I made fettuccine Alfredo."

"Oh, yum! I love Italian."

"Good, because this would be even more awkward if you didn't like Italian."

"No tomatoes though, right?" she asked.

"I swear. Relax." He disappeared into the galley.

Alexis leaned back against the chair and stared out at all the boats and lights in the marina, wondering what was in store for her.

And wondering what she had got herself into with a man like this.

They had a great, easygoing and relaxing dinner. Alexis couldn't remember the last time she'd felt so at ease with someone she'd just met. They talked a bit about their respective jobs and other nonsensical things, but it was the kind of stuff that would help convince anyone who would question them about their marriage, that they were in fact a legitimate couple.

The only problem was…they weren't.

She meant what she'd said before, that she would like to be his friend, even after all this was done. She was enjoying Marcus's company.

It had been a long time since she'd been on a first date.

It's not really a date.

After the dinner was over, they headed up on deck to enjoy the evening breeze and listen to the faint noises of Pillsbury Sound.

"You know," he said, finally breaking the silence that had fallen between them. "You could just scoot over to the British Virgin Islands."

"I could, but then I wouldn't be able to return to the US Virgin Islands to work, and Pepper couldn't come to me. My patients are here in the United States. I have to be here with them."

Marcus nodded. "I understand that."

"No matter what way I do this, I'm putting

myself in jeopardy, but it's worth it. I don't want to go back to England again."

"Because of your ex?"

"Not just him," she said softly.

She didn't want to talk about her loneliness there. And she didn't want to talk about her parents. There was nothing for her in the United Kingdom, but there was everything here for her, and this is where she wanted to stay.

St. John felt like home.

"Believe me, I understand. I don't want to return to mainland US and in particular not California. It holds too many bad memories. I went to the mainland because of schooling. I thought that I would like it there better, but I missed the islands. I missed the culture that I grew up with. This is home."

Alexis nodded, a lump forming in her throat. She was getting far too emotional, and she had to put some distance between the two of them. She didn't want to cry, which she seemed to do a lot lately, in front of Marcus.

Even though she was enjoying his company immensely, she wasn't going to be vulnerable to him. She wasn't going to be vulnerable to any man again.

"I think I need to call it a night. I'm exhausted."

"I can take you home."

"Thanks. So, what do we do now? Do you know our next steps?"

"Well, I think we have to go to the superior court on St. Thomas and apply for a marriage license. You'll have to bring your divorce decree. And dress nice—formal. They don't tolerate casual wear at the courthouse."

Alexis nodded. "Okay. I can do that."

"I'll take us over on the *Tryphine* tomorrow. I have a berth on St. Thomas."

Alexis nodded again, feeling extremely nervous. There was a knot in the pit of her stomach, and she began to wring her hands together. He reached out and took her hands in his.

"It'll be okay," he said, his voice reassuring.

"Are you sure?"

He smiled that half smile. "No, but I've agreed to help you and try. I choose to remain optimistic."

She smiled at him. "Okay. I'll be optimistic too."

Although she still wasn't sure this was the right idea, there was no denying that Marcus was a gem. He was so nice, but she worried she was ruining his life by allowing him to go ahead with this marriage.

And that was the last thing she wanted to do.

CHAPTER FOUR

MARCUS SHOULD HAVE gone and picked up Alexis himself, but he had to stay and ready the *Tryphine* for departure. She'd assured him last night, when he dropped her off, that he didn't need to come pick her up—she was perfectly capable of walking—but he still felt bad.

He felt like he needed to take care of her.

You're just worried about saying "I do."

Marcus tugged on his collar. It was a bit stifling. He hated wearing suits at the best of times, but today it felt like his tie and his collar were choking him like a noose.

He took another deep breath.

"You look dapper," Chase called out as he walked up the gangplank. He was dressed in a suit as well. They needed a witness to pull off this marriage, and since this was Chase and Pepper's brilliant idea, Chase had been volunteered.

"Thanks. I hate this, by the way," Marcus grumbled as he adjusted a knot on the rigging.

"I know, but you have no idea what this means to me, to Pepper…to our family."

Marcus smiled at Chase. "Thank goodness my boat is motorized so I can take her across without sailing. I'm not supposed to be doing any 'jigging,' as Vic puts it."

"Isn't jigging dancing?"

"Yes, and I think you jig squid too, but I'd guess that none of that is allowed either."

Chase chuckled. "What're you going to tell Matthew and Vic?"

"About what?"

"Your marriage?" Chase asked.

Marcus frowned. He hadn't really thought about telling his brother. He had briefly let it pass through his mind, knowing that his brother would not approve of it, but that had been when he was just barely entertaining the idea. Now they were going across to St. Thomas to get a license and marry in front of a judge.

He couldn't hide this for the next two years.

He would have to tell Matthew and Victoria about it, though he had no idea how or what he was going to tell them exactly.

Hey, this is my fake wife. I'm putting my medical license and freedom in jeopardy to commit fraud because Chase and Pepper asked me nicely.

It wasn't the most eloquent way of putting it.

Marcus didn't want to lie to Matthew. Since the domino surgery, they had been on a path to healing their relationship. They were trying to reconnect and if Marcus lied to his brother now, it could ruin the tenuous relationship they currently had, but on the flip side, Marcus didn't want a lot of people knowing that his marriage to Alexis was fake. If too many people knew that this was a marriage of convenience, then what they were doing here was a moot point.

Alexis would be deported.

Pepper would be in trouble, facing a risky birth without the one midwife she trusted to see her through it, and Marcus would most likely lose his medical license and face jail time.

What would his parents think about that?

It was bad enough that he mostly felt like

he was the disappointment in the family. His parents and Matthew had told him time and time again that he wasn't, but there was still a part of him that felt like he could never live up to their expectations.

"I guess I'm going to have to tell Matthew," Marcus said, finally answering the question. The real question though was just how much he was going to tell his twin.

"No point in lying. You've got to rip the Band-Aid off sooner or later."

"You're full of bright ideas," Marcus groused.

"I am. So, when do we leave?"

"As soon as Alexis gets here."

"Here she comes now," Chase said, walking by as Marcus finished some of the more difficult tasks so that they could get underway.

Marcus glanced up and saw Alexis walk toward the mooring, and his breath caught in his throat at the sight of her. The world around him melted away as he just stared at the woman. Her honey hair was down in those soft waves that he loved. The flowy summer dress hit all the right curves, and he let his gaze wander over each and every one, even the swell of the life she carried under her heart.

She's not yours.

He climbed down and helped her on board, taking her tiny, delicate hand in his.

"Sorry, my hands are a bit rough."

"No doubt from all that pirating work," she quipped.

He chuckled. "Too right."

"Sorry I'm late," she apologized.

"You're not late. We'll get there in plenty of time."

"Oh, good."

"You look lovely," he said, and he hoped that his voice didn't shake as he said it.

That peachy pink he liked so much flooded her cheeks. "Thank you. You look very dashing yourself."

"I try," he teased, winking as he helped get her settled on deck. "We'll be leaving soon. It's a short trip to St. Thomas."

"How are you going to manage sailing when you're still recovering?" she asked.

"The *Tryphine* has a motor, so it isn't so much an all-hands-on-deck situation today."

"I was hoping to swashbuckle a bit this morning."

"Again with the pirate metaphor?" he asked.

She laughed. "I'm sorry. I promise it's the last one. I just can't help it."

He laughed. "I can see that."

Chase came back on deck and greeted Alexis before helping Marcus finish preparing the boat to leave. They slipped their moorings and headed out of the marina toward the open waters of the Caribbean Sea, leaving Cruz Bay behind them. The sun was bright, with big white clouds in the blue sky, and the water was calm, with only little whitecaps, as they sailed toward St. Thomas.

Marcus drank in the feel of the sun on his face. It felt good to get back out on the open water. This was what he loved to do. Just him and the *Tryphine*. Other than helping others by being a doctor, this was all he needed out of life.

And as much as he loved his home in the US Virgin Islands, there was a very small part of him that wanted to take the risk and set out on a world tour. Just him, his boat and the open sea.

Marcus had dreamed about it for some time, but he didn't know what was holding him back. The only thing he could think was that Dawna had always thought it was a silly idea to travel the world by boat, and her scorn had caused him to push the dream to the far corners of his mind.

She'd always favored vacations in five-star resorts, not that there was anything wrong with that, but it wasn't what Marcus really wanted. He wanted to take some time and really see the world. He wanted to get to know the people of faraway lands, and you couldn't really do that staying a five-star resort.

He glanced down at Alexis and smiled to himself as he watched her. She was glowing as she looked over the prow of the *Tryphine*. Marcus was in awe of her.

She'd come here after her marriage ended, pregnant and alone. Alexis had taken a huge chance and was taking another chance now doing whatever it took to stay here. Marcus admired her for that and couldn't help but wonder if he should take a leaf out of her book and go on his adventure for a year, once their marriage had ended.

Who would look after your patients then?

That thought sobered him.

He wouldn't let them down.

He couldn't let them down.

St. Thomas came into view just then, and as they rounded the island they headed toward Charlotte Amalie, the beautiful town filled with brightly roofed houses clinging to the side of lush green hills. A horn blared across the water as a cruise ship slowly made its way into port.

"Oh, wow!" Alexis gasped.

Marcus smiled at her wonder as she took it all in.

"It's great, right?"

Alexis nodded. "I've always wanted to see the world via ship or boat. This is just heaven."

His heart skipped a beat, because he understood what she meant when she said it was heaven. He agreed. Other than saving lives and helping his patients, this was a high he would never get tired of—being at the mercy to the water, the wind, the tide.

It was the rhythm of life.

It was part of who he was.

Marcus guided the yacht to his mooring in Frenchtown in Charlotte Amalie. It was close to the restaurant where Matthew and Victoria had had their supposed work dinner when she'd first arrived and they'd been reunited. Marcus knew now that Vic and Matthew had been lovers years before Matthew married his late wife, Kirsten. Vic had seen the *Tryphine* at its Charlotte Amalie mooring, which annoyed his twin because Matthew had thought Marcus had returned to St. John.

It made him chuckle to himself.

The little bistro was beautiful, and maybe he could get Matthew to pull some strings and he could take Alexis there tonight for an intimate dinner after they got married. They'd be alone as Chase was planning to head back to St. John on the ferry.

Chase helped him tie the boat up and soon he was helping Alexis down the gangplank, while Chase went out to hire a cab to take them to the superior court. Marcus would usually walk to it, but with him still recovering and Alexis six months pregnant, he didn't want to force either of them to walk in this heat.

It was a warm and sunny day, and he was already regretting his suit. He felt like he was melting in it.

They crammed into the back of the tiny cab, Chase leaning forward to speak with the driver and Marcus pressed up against Alexis. Instinctively he put his arm around her shoulders, and she didn't move away. It was nice having her pressed against him; it felt natural.

"It's busy today," she said, her voice shaking slightly.

"The tourists are coming in off the ships. I forgot about that. Tuesday is a particularly busy day at port."

The cab navigated the narrow streets from Frenchtown to the superior court and Chase paid the driver, as Marcus and Alexis were in this predicament because of him. Marcus helped Alexis out of the cab, and they made their way into the courthouse.

Chase had a friend who worked there and had cleared everything for them so they had already arranged an appointment with the judge. And it didn't hurt that Marcus had given his kidney to Mrs. Van Luven, who had worked at the court as a clerk and was still well loved in the court office.

It made him feel all the more guilty for deceiving them, but he was here now to marry Alexis and there was no going back.

Alexis was nervous. She'd been so isolated in her little world at the midwife practice. She went to work and then went back to the dorm room near the clinic. Sometimes she'd go to the little market to get something to eat, but it had been four months since she'd been out in a big, bustling city with a lot of people around her.

She'd forgotten what a busy city was like, and it was a bit nerve racking to be in such a crush of people. Alexis never did like crowds. They made her feel as though she was suffocating.

Bruce had loved parties and people.

Often, she would spend her whole time at a party alone in a corner or glued to Bruce's side and bored out of her mind. He used to tease her about being such a wallflower or leaning on him, but Marcus didn't say anything.

As if he sensed her trepidation, he pulled her closer.

Although she should've shied away from him, she didn't. She was glad that she could lean on Marcus, and it felt good to have his arm around her. She felt safe, like she'd known him her whole life, which made her feel bad that he was part of this ruse. Maybe it would be easier if she didn't like him so much?

It would be easier on her to stay away from him, but she liked being with him.

He'd looked so handsome steering his boat across the channel to St. Thomas, like he belonged on the water, and it was amazing to have the wind in her face.

She could only imagine what it would be like to be out on open water and have the sails out. To see nothing but sea, sails and sky. The baby fluttered inside her and reminded her that she had to stay grounded.

It was her baby and the kind of life she wanted her baby to have that had brought her here to this moment, and she couldn't be greedy. Even if she wanted to be.

The courthouse was a bit calmer, but it was still busy for a Tuesday morning. She let Chase and Marcus lead her to where she needed to go, barely able to pay attention to where they were going as she was so overwhelmed by sensations.

"Do you have your divorce decree?" Marcus asked, interrupting her thoughts.

"What? Yes." She reached into her purse and pulled out the documents. She wasn't sure when they had arrived at the counter to get their license.

The woman working there inputted the information and handed Marcus more paperwork with instructions to wait in the chairs until their names were called.

Alexis's heart was hammering, and she placed a hand on her chest as she took deep breaths, trying to calm her frayed nerves.

She swore, after what happened with Bruce, that she would never do this again. She would never get married and yet here she was, waiting to get married. Marcus filled out his information and Alexis filled out hers. A short time later they were called in to do a brief preceremony interview to ensure they were both willingly entering into the union, and then they were told to wait once again to be called in for their wedding ceremony.

She still couldn't quite believe she was doing this. She was putting a lot at risk.

Marcus was too. Just to help her.

It weighed heavily on her, and she suddenly felt like she was going to have a panic attack.

"Olesen and Martin?" a clerk called.

"That's us." There was an edge to Marcus's voice as he took her hand and they headed to the chambers. Alexis's pulse thundered between her ears, and she felt like she was going to faint.

The judge entered the room.

He was an older man; his face was extremely red and he was sweating.

Profusely.

Alexis cocked her head, concerned. Besides the bloodred coloring in his cheeks and the sweat across his brow, his pallor was gray.

She'd seen this happen before, when she worked in an accident and emergency department in an inner-city hospital in London, and she couldn't tear her eyes from his face. All her mental alarms were going off that something was very wrong.

"This is a pretty standard procedure," the judge said through gasping breaths.

Marcus glanced at her, and she could tell by the way his brow was furrowed that he was concerned too.

The judge started to read the script, and in no time at all he reached the vows.

"Marcus Olesen, do you take Alexis Martin in matrimony?" the judge asked.

"I do," Marcus answered.

"And do you, Alexis Martin, take Marcus Olesen in matrimony?"

Alexis swallowed the lump in her throat. Her stomach was doing flip-flops. She felt like this was the biggest mistake.

What're you doing?

"I do."

"Then, by the powers vested in me by the United States Virgin Islands, I now pronounce you husband and wife." The judge's voice began to slur on the final word, and his face was drooping as he quickly signed the marriage certificate and then handed it over for each of them to sign. The paperwork all complete, he stamped it and moved to hand it over, but Alexis and Marcus watched in horror as the judge grabbed his arm holding the certificate, grimaced, cried out and then toppled over.

Marcus dove for the judge, and Alexis flung open the door as Chase helplessly watched on. "Someone call an ambulance. The judge has collapsed!"

"Alexis, are the paramedics on the way?" Marcus asked a few minutes later as he continued to administer CPR to the judge.

"Yes." Alexis was seeing if she could find what she needed in the first-aid kit.

"Blast," Marcus cursed. "His throat is closing. He's not getting oxygen."

"What do you need?" Alexis asked.

"Surgical kit," Marcus said grimly. "If they have one."

Alexis pressed her lips together and dug through the first-aid box. Thankfully, it was well stocked, in case of an emergency like a hurricane. At the very bottom of the box, she found a simple surgical kit. "How is this?" She handed him the kit.

"It's fine."

"What're you thinking?"

"Tracheotomy," Marcus stated. "He can't breathe. His throat is closed."

Alexis knelt beside Marcus, who slipped off his jacket and rolled up his sleeves.

"I'm going to need your help, Alexis," Marcus said. "It's been a while since I've done one."

"Same," Alexis said. "But tell me what to do."

Marcus nodded and she opened the kit, handing him gloves and Betadine. Alexis put on gloves and watched as Marcus found the cricoid cartilage, just under the Adam's apple.

She handed Marcus the scalpel.

He made the incision, and Alexis prepared a straw she found in the judge's desk as a makeshift breathing tube.

"Here." She handed him the straw.

He smiled. "Good thinking."

Marcus inserted the straw and leaned over to breathe through it twice before continuing his chest compressions. The judge was still not breathing, so Marcus continued giving rescue breaths through the tube and performing CPR.

Finally the paramedics arrived, and Marcus helped them load the judge onto the gurney. He then continued with his compressions and breaths.

"Where should we take him, Dr. Olesen?" the paramedic asked.

"Ziese Memorial and be sure to page my brother, Dr. Olesen."

Alexis and Chase stood back as Marcus prepared to leave with the paramedics to go to the hospital.

"What should we do now?" Alexis asked.

"Well, we should probably go to Ziese Memorial. I think you and Marcus need to go to Immigration together, and that's kind of hard to do when your new husband is helping to save a life," Chase said.

Alexis chuckled. "Let's go then."

Chase hailed a cab, and it was a short ride across town to Ziese Memorial from the courthouse. Alexis could hear the wail of the siren as the cab followed closely behind.

The hospital was new and built, like all the other buildings in town, against the side of the hill, with a bright red roof and white plaster walls. It looked like one of those typical island hospitals, but Alexis knew that this was a state-of-the-art building.

It was the kind of hospital she would love to work at. And she knew from the domino that had recently been performed that they were the top of their game in the Caribbean.

Alexis stared around in wonder at it all.

"Can I help you?" a volunteer asked.

"I'm looking for Dr. Olesen." Alexis flashed her identification, showing that she was a nurse. It was an old habit to always carry it with her.

The volunteer smiled and nodded. "Follow me."

Alexis followed the volunteer who took her down through some halls that led out onto the surgical floor. She was worried about the judge, and the fact that they'd brought him straight to the surgical floor meant his condition was a lot more serious than she'd initially thought.

"He's right over there," the volunteer said, pointing across the room to where Marcus, in scrubs, was standing with his back to her talking with someone. She was surprised to see him in scrubs already, but not shocked as his brother was the chief of surgery and he'd just performed an emergency tracheotomy.

She'd been so impressed with his calm, collected head through the whole ordeal.

Marcus continued to impress and amaze her. He was like no man she'd ever met before.

Marcus was one of a kind.

"Thank goodness I found you. I have the marriage certificate. How is the judge doing?" Alexis asked.

The man turned around and though the blue eyes—wide with shock—were the same, there was no beard and she could tell straight-away that this was Marcus's brother.

Apparently, Marcus hadn't thought it worth mentioning that his brother was his identical twin.

"I'm sorry?" he asked.

"You're not Marcus." She took a step back, mortified.

"No. I'm not. I'm his brother, Matthew," he said carefully as he assessed her. "And you are?"

"Alexis Martin. I'm a nurse practitioner and midwife."

"You said something about a marriage certificate... Are you telling me you're my brother's wife?"

Alexis worried her bottom lip. She had really stepped into it, and she only hoped that Marcus wasn't too annoyed with her that she'd let it slip.

"Yes. I am."

CHAPTER FIVE

MARCUS HAD TO continue to administer CPR in the ambulance and was up on the gurney with the patient as the paramedics wheeled him into the emergency room.

"Can someone please explain to me why my donor patient is straddling and treating a suspected stroke patient?"

Marcus cringed hearing his sister-in-law's voice boom across the emergency room.

When they finally had the judge in a pod, he was able to get off and hand over the compressions to the residents and the trauma team.

Marcus was still a bit shocked that minutes after the judge had pronounced him and Alexis as husband and wife he had been cutting open the man's throat to save his life.

Now he was in trouble with his surgeon.

"I didn't think that transplant surgeons

graced the emergency room floor," Marcus teased after he signed over the judge to the ER team.

Vic crossed her arms and raised one eyebrow in question. "We do when one of her patients comes in. I just didn't expect to see *you* here."

"Is your patient okay?" Marcus asked.

"Fine. I'm wondering how you're doing." She took a step back. "You're in a suit. What were you doing at the superior court anyway?"

"How do you know I was at the courthouse?" Marcus asked.

Victoria pointed. "The judge?"

Marcus grinned. "Are you always this bossy with Matthew?"

She chuckled. "More, but seriously you're not even cleared to practice yet. What were you doing?"

"Saving a man's life?"

Victoria smiled. "Okay, but still, you have to be careful."

"Well…" Marcus trailed off and he glanced up to see his brother marching across the emergency room toward them, followed by Alexis, who looked worried.

Oh, no.

His stomach knotted and fell to the bottom of his feet. Actually, lower than that. It felt like he was walking around on it. Digging his heels into it. This was not how he wanted his brother to find out.

I'm sorry, Alexis mouthed behind Matthew, who stood in front of Marcus with his arms crossed.

"Hi, Matthew," Marcus said cheerfully.

Victoria was looking worried now. "What's going on?"

"Marcus is married," Matthew announced.

Victoria's eyes widened and she took a step back. "What?"

Marcus stepped forward and took Alexis's hand. "This is my wife, Alexis Martin. She's a nurse practitioner and a midwife on St. John, and we were married this afternoon. That's why I was at the superior court."

Alexis waved nervously.

"It's lovely to meet you!" Victoria stepped forward and hugged them both awkwardly. Then she stepped back and nudged Matthew.

"Welcome to the family," Matthew said, giving Alexis a hug and then shaking Marcus's hand. "I'm sorry for seeming a bit surprised. I didn't even know Marcus was dating anyone."

"Yeah, well, you've been a bit preoccupied, brother, with your new wife."

Matthew grinned and looked warmly at Victoria. "This is true."

Victoria sighed. "This isn't the best place to get to know one another."

Matthew nodded. "How about dinner tonight at our place?"

Marcus opened his mouth to decline, but Alexis nodded and said, "That sounds lovely. Thank you."

So much for his plan to have an intimate dinner alone. Though maybe dinner with this brother and Victoria would be better than tempting fate by spending more time alone with Alexis.

"Great," Victoria said. "How about six? Kind of early, but we're working until then."

"It's fine. We have some other business to attend to." Marcus took Alexis's hand. "We'll see you both tonight."

He escorted Alexis out of the emergency room of Ziese Memorial and didn't say anything to her until they were outside.

"I thought Chase was with you?" Marcus asked.

"He was, but then we got separated and

someone asked if they could help me. I figured it was the easiest way to find you."

Marcus ran a hand through his hair. "Well, I wanted to tell my brother. I just didn't expect you would be the one to actually do it."

"I thought he was you from behind," Alexis whispered. "You didn't tell me that your brother was an identical twin!"

He couldn't fault her on that as he hadn't told her that bit of information. He began to laugh thinking about what a shock it must've been for his brother.

"What's so funny?" Alexis asked.

"I was just picturing Matthew's face. What did you say to him exactly?"

Alexis smiled. "I said something about our marriage license. I can't remember exactly. He was a bit shocked, and when he turned around and I saw that it wasn't you, it furthered his shock. I don't think that he expected you were going to get married."

"Trust me, I understand his shock. It was never in my plans either."

It had been at one time, long ago when he'd been in love with a woman who he thought had loved him back. He'd been an absolute fool. So no, he didn't think marriage was for him, and he was only doing this out of the goodness of his heart.

This wasn't real.

Chase came running out of the hospital just then and came to an abrupt stop beside them. "Sorry, I went to look for intake and then I turned around and Alexis was gone. I'm glad you two found each other. How is the judge?"

Marcus frowned. "I don't know. He was handed off to the trauma surgeons. Alexis and I have been invited to dinner at my brother's house later tonight. Maybe he'll tell us then."

Chase's eyes widened. "So he knows, then."

"He knows we're married," Alexis said quickly. "He doesn't know about the other part."

Chase nodded in understanding. "Gotcha. So what're you two going to do now?"

Marcus had no idea. It was several hours before he and Alexis were scheduled to have dinner with Victoria and Matthew, so the day was theirs. He wasn't sure what married couples did, beyond the obvious of what married couples tended to do... And he didn't want to think about that.

Not that he wouldn't like that to happen with Alexis, since he was highly attracted to her. It was just, it *couldn't* happen. Alexis was pregnant; she was off-limits. She had made it clear that she was just going to stay married to him so that she could stay in the country. This was not one of his holiday flings.

But suddenly the idea of having one of those kinds of flings again made him a bit queasy.

"Some sightseeing and lunch?" Marcus suggested. "What're you going to do?" he asked Chase.

"I'll catch the Cruz Bay ferry back to St. John. I don't like leaving Pepper alone for very long, and Jonas is still recovering. He's fine here, but I'm glad he'll be coming home soon!"

"That's great! Be safe," Marcus said, clapping his best friend on the back and pulling him into a hug.

"Thanks again, you two." Chase briefly hugged Alexis and then hailed a cab to take him down to the ferry wharf.

It was just Marcus and Alexis now.

They were alone.

And he didn't want to stand outside a hospital killing time.

"What would you like to do?"

"I don't know. Since I got here I haven't

had much time for sightseeing. I've just been working and dealing with morning sickness." She touched her belly gently, and Marcus fought the urge to reach out and touch her.

He didn't know what came over him in that moment that made him want to do that. It wasn't like he was going to be a part of the child's life.

"Well, most of the historic and touristy places will be teeming with tourists from the big cruise ships. Would you like to rent a car and go for a drive? Get away from the hustle and bustle of downtown Charlotte Amalie? I mean, the embassy is closed right now for lunch, so we have time to kill."

Alexis nodded. "Yes, I would like that very much, but do let me pay for it. You made me dinner the other night and brought me here."

"I'm the one that has a valid license for the Virgin Islands, and we drive on the right here."

She smiled and nodded. "Okay, but the next time I will take care of it."

"Next time?" He couldn't help but ask.

She blushed. "You know, in case we get a visit from Immigration or something. We'll have to present a united front for a while."

"How? It's a fake marriage."

"I know, but if anyone comes calling to check up on me, we'll have to…"

"Be in this together," he said, finishing off her sentence.

"Precisely."

"You're right." He cleared his throat.

"So what do we do?"

She worried her bottom lip. "I haven't quite thought it through."

"Well, we can start by some sightseeing. You stay here, and I'll go rent us a car. There's a car rental place not far from here."

Marcus had to put some distance between them. Even just for a moment. His pulse was racing, and he got so excited when she mentioned a next time. He was acting like he was a young man again, in that first flush of love and not the hardened, jaded playboy that he had become.

It wasn't long of a wait before Marcus pulled up in a small convertible, and Alexis couldn't contain her excitement when the little red car came to a stop beside her, with its top down. It was the kind of car that one should travel in when visiting an island paradise.

Or at least that was her opinion.

Marcus parked and got out of the car to

open her door. She couldn't remember any man doing that for her, and just that simple gentlemanly act made her swoon just a bit. He really was the perfect package.

After he closed the door, he climbed into the driver's seat. "All buckled up?"

"Yep. I'm ready." She was more than ready to go on an adventure. She didn't care where they went. It would just be nice to see more of one of the islands.

Marcus headed up a winding road in a northeastern direction, away from Ziese Memorial Hospital. There was a lot of traffic headed in the same direction, and she remembered reading that a lot of people chose to get married at the beaches that lined Magens Bay.

A beach wedding sounded nice.

Although the strange and surreal wedding that she and Marcus had had in the judge's office at the superior court before the judge collapsed was one they would be sure to talk about for some time.

Some time?

There would be no some time with Marcus. Why was it so easy for her to forget that?

As the little red convertible wound its way up the hill, Marcus pulled into a turnout that had angled parking and a railing. She gasped when he parked the car and they could see Charlotte Amalie laid out below them, along with the sea, clouds and massive cruise ships in the harbor.

It was like something from a postcard. This was what she always pictured when she dreamed of the islands.

It was like stepping into that dream.

"Oh, wow! This is amazing."

"It's cool, right?"

Alexis undid her seat belt and got out of the car, not waiting for Marcus to open the door. She wandered to the edge of the railing and just drank in the sight of paradise from above. Marcus came and leaned against the railing next to her.

They didn't say anything. Just stared out at the city below them.

"You know, we didn't get to seal the deal."

"Seal the deal?" she asked, confused.

"The judge never got to the part where he says we can kiss, because he collapsed."

Her stomach did a flip. "He did sign the certificate though. We are still legally married."

"Yes, but the bride and groom always kiss after they're married and we didn't."

She'd been thinking about that too. When

it was coming to that part, she got so nervous and she wasn't sure how she was going to handle the situation. It would look bad if she didn't kiss Marcus, but the idea of kissing him made her nervous.

And even thinking about it right now, as they stared out over Charlotte Amalie and the turquoise sea below them, her mouth went dry and her pulse raced. She had wanted to kiss him too, but Alexis felt it was too late. The moment to do it had passed.

She cleared her throat and stepped away from the railing.

And from him.

She needed to put distance between them.

"I really do hope the judge pulls through."

Not that she wanted to think about the judge in that moment, but it was a way to break the tension that she was feeling. It was a way to break the spell so she could step away.

"Me as well," Marcus said, standing up straight instead of leaning over the rail. "Well, we should carry on."

"Where to?" she asked, intrigued. "I thought this was it."

He gave her a look as if to say, come on. "A turnout at the side of the road is no way to kill a lot of time. It's a nice distraction, but do you think so little of me?"

It was a tease.

"Sorry." She laughed nervously. "I didn't mean to insult your honorable intentions for killing time before our awkward dinner with your twin and his wife."

Now it was Marcus's turn to laugh as he opened the car door for her. "Well, that's one way of putting it."

"I still feel extremely bad for spilling that news to your brother. You should have been the one to tell him. It wasn't my place," she said as he climbed back into the car.

"I was going to tell him. Honestly, I wish I had been there to see his face. That's the part I missed, the part I feel cheated out of." He grinned deviously.

"Well, he was certainly surprised."

"I can only imagine. And so I will keep trying to picture it. It'll bring me joy." He grinned and she laughed.

"That sounds mean."

"It's not. Not really. Not anymore. We spent so many years at odds that we, in a way, forgot to be brothers for a while. I guess it's a force of habit to be mean to one another."

"I wouldn't know. I don't have any siblings.

My childhood was quite lonely, really." She found herself reaching down to touch her belly. Her child would never feel the loneliness that she had. Her lonely childhood had nothing to do with being an only child. It had more to do with her emotionally distant parents. It scared her, because there were times that Alexis wondered if she was actually genetically capable of emotion.

Of love.

She wasn't taught those things. It was one of Bruce's problems in their relationship, and she saw it now. He didn't think that she was loving enough. He was always annoyed that she didn't fawn over him, didn't cling to him.

Of course, what Bruce really wanted was a damsel in distress, which she was anything but. Still, she was scared that she wouldn't be able to be as demonstrative as she wanted to be and that her child would feel they lacked for love.

That's just fear talking. You know that.

Alexis had wanted this child so badly. She yearned to hold a piece of her heart and she was thrilled to be pregnant, even though it scared her to do this alone without support from anyone.

There had been so many times that she'd

longed for a hug from her mother, but her mother was so self-absorbed and her father was always working. She couldn't count on anyone, but she was going to be here for her child. Even though it was just her, her child would never feel alone. Single parenthood might be difficult for her to navigate, but her child was going to know that it was loved. It might just be the two of them, but Alexis would make sure it was more than enough.

"I'm sorry to hear that," Marcus said, intruding on her thoughts.

Alexis shrugged. "I was lucky in other ways. I was educated, fed and safe."

"What about loved?" he asked softly.

"I'd like to think so, but my parents aren't very… They don't show it. They're a bit controlling. A bit cold."

And, of course, her mother thought that pleasing one's husband was enough in life. It seemed so unhappy, so sad to live that way. To only live to please another person. But that was her mother's life, and her mother's choice.

Not hers.

"Well, I have a beautiful place we can walk through and enjoy. Somewhere to take our minds off all of it," he said brightly.

He slowed down near a gate on a dirt road, which had a sign advertising botanical gardens and a tea shop. Over the hedges Alexis could see the peak of greenhouses.

"Oh!" she exclaimed. "A garden sounds lovely."

"I thought you might like this. It's quiet, we can get some shade and they have a lovely tea shop in the center where we can get some lunch."

"Good choice."

"I'm glad you approve. My late sister-in-law loved this place."

Alexis noticed he said this with a hint of sadness in his voice. "Your late sister-in-law? Do you have another sibling?"

Marcus shook his head. "No, Matthew was married before, and his wife, Kirsten, died of cancer at quite a young age. When Matthew was working and she was feeling down, I would bring her here. She loved looking at the orchids and watching the birds."

"Sounds like you cared for her a great deal."

Marcus nodded. "Victoria is great too. She brought my brother back to life and she did save my life during the domino when I developed a blood clot in surgery, so I kind of owe her that."

Marcus winked and Alexis smiled.

He was such a kind soul. His kindness made her swoon, and she didn't understand why he was still single. How could any woman let a man like this get away?

Aren't you planning on doing that when this is done?

She shook that thought away as Marcus parked the car. This time Alexis paid the entrance fee, and they wound their way through the quiet gardens and straight to the conservatory that had the tearoom, which she was glad for. The gardens were beautiful, but she was tired and parched.

They found a table in the corner, next to a bubbly waterfall, and ordered simple tea with little sandwiches. Alexis leaned back in her chair and watched the water falling over the rocks and burbling at the bottom.

A parrot sat on a perch nearby, preening itself, and her stress began to melt away as she listened to the sounds of nature around her.

"So tomorrow we hit Immigration and the embassies?" Marcus asked.

Alexis nodded. "Yes. Hand in our paperwork, I suppose."

"Why is it so awkward between us again?" he asked.

"I don't know. I mean, we don't know much about each other and now we're married. And I'm pregnant. We haven't really talked about that either."

Marcus took a deep breath. "And we'll need to. Matthew and Victoria will want to know. It is sort of the elephant in the room and one of the reasons we got married, in a roundabout way."

"Exactly." She worried her bottom lip. "I don't know what to say."

"I can say it's mine. I mean, we'll be married for some time, so people will assume…"

Alexis's breath caught in her throat. Bruce didn't want his child, but here was a man she barely knew who was offering to claim her baby. Even though it secretly thrilled her, she couldn't let him do that.

"I can't let you. When we get divorced, what will you tell your brother and his wife when you have no custody rights?"

"I would tell them the truth. By then you'd be a US citizen."

A lump formed in her throat. "I hate that you have to be involved in this deception. I can't let you do this."

She was moved that Marcus saw the solution so black-and-white, but she didn't see it that way. There was a part of her that didn't trust him. Bruce had signed away his rights to their child, but she didn't want Marcus to try and claim rights down the road either.

Not that she expected he would, but she had to be careful.

She'd been burned and hurt one too many times, and Alexis didn't give her trust over so easily. There was a part of her that wanted to trust Marcus, but she couldn't.

"I have no problem. My brother would question me to the point of insanity if I told him the truth now. Me saying the baby is mine is less of a headache for me, but if I have to sign something or swear some kind of oath that I claim no rights, then I'll do that. We just need to present a united front on this so Immigration has no questions."

"Good point."

"So, on that point, I think it's prudent that we move in together."

Marcus couldn't believe the words when they came out of his mouth, until they were slipping past his lips.

What're you thinking?

That was the point. He wasn't thinking. It seemed that when he was around Alexis, he forgot himself. This was supposed to just be a marriage on paper.

Living together was more than just a business arrangement.

He had let himself get swept up with her, and that hadn't happened to him since Dawna. It scared him, but on the flip side, he found he'd missed this sort of connection with someone.

It was making him realize how lonely he had been for a really long time.

It still didn't register with him right away that he'd just asked Alexis to move in with him.

The *Tryphine* was a large sailboat, but it was still confined quarters with a woman who was off-limits and whom he was highly attracted to. On top of all that, she was pregnant with another man's baby. Although that fool had given up his child. What an idiot.

"Sorry, did I just hear you correctly? You want me to move in with you?" she asked, shocked.

"Well, we are married, and again, we need to keep up appearances."

Alexis's eyes were still wide, and she blinked a couple of times. "Yes, but…"

"But what? We're both putting a lot on the line to do this, so it only makes sense we live together."

"I suppose."

"And you live in a temporary residence, so I can't move in there with you."

"No, you can't. I just have a small room. It's tight quarters."

"There are two bedrooms on the *Tryphine*. I have room for you."

Alexis nodded. "Okay…yes, you're right, and it's only temporary."

The waitress brought their light lunch and tea just then, but as Marcus bit into a cucumber sandwich it tasted like sawdust in his mouth. Even his taste buds were rebelling against his bonkers idea to have her move in with him, but he knew it ultimately made perfect sense.

And even though she was worried about the deception of the baby being his and even though he told her it was no big deal, he did feel bad for lying to Matthew and Victoria. He was also envious of Matthew. Not many people knew yet, but Victoria was currently pregnant with their first child. Matthew had what Marcus had wanted years ago with Dawna—a family.

They finished their lunch and took a walk around the gardens. Marcus found it a bit boring, but it was a place to kill time before they had to head back to Charlotte Amalie for dinner at his brother's place.

Something he was dreading.

"I need to sit down for a moment," Alexis said. Her face was flushed, but not with heat. It immediately fired off his red flags that something was wrong.

Marcus guided her to a bench. Out of instinct, he touched her face and checked her pulse, which was quite sluggish.

"How far along are you?" he asked.

"Twenty-six weeks."

"I know you're a midwife, but have you been tested for gestational diabetes? Do you track your ketones and protein?"

"I do. My protein has been a bit high, but I've been busy and stressed." She closed her eyes and took a deep breath.

He frowned. "We're going back to Ziese Memorial."

"I'm just overheated."

"So nurses are also bad patients too."

"How do mean?" she asked, confused.

"That old saying that doctors make the worst patients, well, the same goes for you. I've treated pregnant patients before they head off to their OB/GYN. I know what I'm talking about, and I know you know what you need to do. We're going to Charlotte Amalie, and we're going to get some tests done."

Marcus wasn't taking no for an answer. Alexis was stressed, but he was worried her stress had caught up with her and she'd missed the signs. She was awfully small too for how many weeks she was along. It was better to be safe than sorry in this situation.

"Okay, you're right. Let's go, Dr. Olesen. Thank you."

He shrugged and took her hand to make sure she didn't fall on the way back to the car. "It's what good husbands do."

CHAPTER SIX

MATTHEW HAD GIVEN Marcus hospital privileges so that his brother could order the tests, and then sent down one of his OB/GYN doctors to assist as Marcus couldn't act as Alexis's doctor since they were married.

It annoyed Marcus, both because Matthew was right and also because Marcus knew the truth. On paper he was Alexis's husband, but he wasn't actually. It also meant that Matthew had found out even more news about Alexis without Marcus being the one to tell him. He was already beginning to dread the conversation he had to have with his brother tonight…

The upcoming dinner was looming over him like some kind of great, big elephant ready to burst, which he knew wasn't the correct analogy, but he was feeling a bit stressed himself and couldn't seem to think of anything more bigger and awkward than an elephant.

Especially an exploding one.

"You're pacing," Alexis murmured from where she was lying down on an exam table.

"Am I?"

"What're you agitated about?"

"Elephants," he groused.

Alexis cocked an eyebrow and sat up. "What? That's an odd thing to be anxious about."

He grinned. "It isn't if it blows up."

"You're an interesting man, Marcus Olesen."

"Interesting is better than boring."

The OB/GYN, Dr. Baxter, came in after knocking. "I have your blood work. I'm going to send you to have a glucose tolerance test done, and you do have some high protein that worries me. Your blood pressure is slightly elevated as well."

Alexis worried her bottom lip, and Marcus instinctively took her hand in his. Alexis didn't pull away and almost seemed to lean into him, which was nice.

"When should I do the glucose test?" Alexis asked. "And can I do it at my clinic on St. John?"

Dr. Baxter nodded. "Yes, at your clinic is fine, but I need you to take it easy and I want to be your physician to monitor this. I would like you to take your blood pressure daily, because if you don't take it easy and it continues to elevate, I am going to put you on bed rest."

"I have to work to stay in the country," Alexis said quickly.

Dr. Baxter looked confused. "Didn't you two just get married? I think that makes your work visa a moot point now."

Alexis's cheeks flushed crimson. "Yes. It does."

And even Marcus held his breath in that moment. He had been worried about little slipups like this.

Thankfully, Dr. Baxter just smiled gently at them. "Besides, with a doctor's note, it wouldn't affect your visa. If you need bed rest, you need bed rest and you do need to take it easier. Now, how about an ultrasound? You're measuring quite small as well."

Alexis nodded, and Marcus helped her lie back down on the exam table. He knew she was worried, and even though he had no connection to the baby or her, he was concerned too.

Dr. Baxter spread the gel on her belly and

Marcus watched the screen. It took a moment before he saw the little black-and-white fetus appear. Even though it wasn't his child and he'd seen ultrasounds before, he felt an instantaneous connection, right then and there, like a bolt of lightning. An awe overtook him that Alexis was carrying a life inside her.

Dr. Baxter smiled. "Everything looks good."

Alexis smiled. "I'm glad to hear that."

Dr. Baxter took some pictures and then wiped the gel off Alexis's belly with a towel. "I'll go book that test for you in Cruz Bay for the end of this week and get you a picture of your baby."

Dr. Baxter left and Alexis sat up.

"I feel like a fool," she muttered.

"Why?" Marcus asked.

"I'm a midwife and a nurse and I didn't see the signs. If I had been paying attention, I would've got the glucose test done earlier."

"Hey, as I said before, medical professionals are the worst patients and you've had a lot going on." He reached out and touched her chin, her skin so soft under his fingers. He felt like his hands were too tough, too clumsy, to touch her delicate skin, but he wanted to feel her.

It was surprising how much he wanted to take her in his arms and protect her.

She leaned forward and rested her forehead against his, her eyes closed.

"Thank you for being here for me," she murmured.

She opened her eyes and as their gazes locked, his pulse started thundering between his ears. She leaned down and kissed him then, a light fleeting kiss on the lips that seared his soul. And then he kissed her back the way he'd wanted to since the moment he met her.

Deeply.

Cupping her face in his hands and losing himself in the softness of her lips.

A knock on the door from Dr. Baxter made him break off the kiss and step back, even though his body was protesting because he wanted more.

So much more.

Alexis was flushed and wouldn't look at him.

Dr. Baxter was a bit oblivious to what had just happened, which was probably a good thing. Marcus wasn't sure what had come over him. He just got swept up in the moment. Which happened a lot when he was around her, now that he thought about it.

And now she was moving in. At his request. It was unsettling.

"The appointment is booked, and here's a picture of your baby. Congratulations again to you both." Dr. Baxter handed them the lab requisition and the picture before leaving.

Alexis didn't look at the picture, but slipped it in her purse.

"Well, I better get cleaned up," she stated.

"Right." Marcus rubbed the back of his neck, trying to calm his pulse. "I'll wait for you in the hall."

Alexis nodded and he slipped out of the room He couldn't seem to control himself when he was near her. He was confused. This was supposed to just be a business arrangement with Alexis. He shouldn't be feeling these emotions.

He shouldn't want her this much.

But he did.

They didn't say much as they left Ziese Memorial Hospital and headed over to Matthew and Victoria's home. Marcus was unusually quiet, and she could feel the tension between them again. And it was no surprise.

A lot had happened.

He'd suggested they move in together. Then he took care of her when she felt sick in the botanical gardens and was there when she saw her baby.

And then she had kissed him when she was at her most vulnerable.

Alexis was still reeling from that kiss.

She didn't know what possessed her to kiss him. She was just caught up in so many emotions, and seeing her baby for the first time had overwhelmed her completely. It was all she could do to keep from crying. Her mother taught her that tears were unladylike, so Alexis had swallowed them back.

Choked them back was more like it—just like she always did—but then she got angry at herself.

Marcus was right about that old saying, that medical professionals made the worst patients. If one of her patients had come into the clinic and presented with symptoms like that, she would've done the same as Dr. Baxter had done. And if she hadn't been so preoccupied with work and stressed about her visa situation, she would've noticed the symptoms sooner.

When she'd kissed Marcus, she'd been

seeking comfort. What surprised her was that he'd kissed her back and kissed her with such intensity it scorched her blood. She had never felt that zing of electricity before.

The hunger for him had been intense.

Alexis was glad Dr. Baxter came back into the room and interrupted them, but she couldn't deny that there was a part of her that had wanted that kiss to continue. She wanted to see where it would lead to.

Alexis was not the one-night-stand type of girl. She was usually the type of woman who played it safe with men. She'd only ever been with Bruce, but the way Marcus had kissed her made her wish she was that type of brave, strong woman who went after what she wanted and who she wanted.

And right now her body still wanted Marcus.

"Here it is," Marcus said, breaking the silence that had fallen between them when they'd left the hospital.

Matthew and Victoria's house was a small little building built up against the hill, not far from the hospital. It had a brightly colored red roof, like so many of the other homes and buildings in Charlotte Amalie, and was nestled against the green of the trees.

"That's quaint," she said. And it wasn't meant disrespectfully; she loved quaint houses.

Marcus grinned. "Quaint? Just wait."

She cocked an eyebrow. "What do you mean by that?"

"You'll see."

"You're frustrating," she teased, relieved as the tension that had been lying heavy between them melted away.

"Sorry, but half the fun is watching people's faces when they see inside this place."

Now she was really curious.

Marcus opened the door and helped her out of the car. The simple touch when she slipped her hand into his sent a zip of heat through her, and she hoped she wasn't blushing. Marcus rang the doorbell and his brother answered it.

"Marcus," Matthew acknowledged.

"Matthew," Marcus said, nodding. "And you remember Alexis?"

Matthew smiled, those same but different eyes twinkling. "A pleasure to see you again, Alexis. Please come in."

Matthew stepped aside to let them in, and as Alexis stepped across the threshold, her mouth dropped open as she took in the beautiful, modern, spacious open concept home. It was a lot larger on the inside than it appeared to be on the outside.

Marcus chuckled and leaned over to whisper. "See?"

"Yes," Alexis murmured back. "I do. Your home is spectacular, Matthew."

He grinned. "Thank you. We are a work in progress. Some minor renovations to prep for when the baby comes."

"Oh! Congratulations," Alexis said. "Marcus didn't tell me."

Matthew snorted. "Not surprising. Of course he didn't really mention anything about you and your baby either."

Her cheeks flushed with warmth.

Marcus put his arm around her reassuringly. "Well, if you remember, dear brother, we haven't exactly been on overly friendly terms until very recently and you've been a wee bit preoccupied with your new job, Vic and the domino."

Matthew laughed. "Fine. You win. You're right."

"Are you two fighting again?" Victoria asked as she came in from the terrace.

"No!" Both Matthew and Marcus answered in unison, glaring at each other.

Victoria shook her head and then smiled warmly at Alexis. "Alexis, welcome."

"Thank you for having us," Alexis said nervously, still recalling the way Victoria had seemed to read right through her. A talent she found really good surgeons and physicians all had. She liked to think that she had that gift too, but having it turned on you was a bit unnerving.

"Our pleasure. I was so pleased when Matthew told me Marcus had gotten married, though it was bit shocking given his surgery was only eight weeks ago." Victoria's gaze was stern, friendly, but meant to strike fear into Marcus who seemed nonplussed about it.

Alexis hoped she wasn't blushing again, but she felt warm.

Victoria was apparently very perceptive, and they were being caught in a lie.

"I read about that surgery. It was impressive," Alexis said, trying to steer the conversation away from her marriage of convenience.

Victoria beamed. "Yes, you must've been worried about Marcus. Though I don't recall seeing you at the hospital."

"What is this?" Marcus asked. "An inquisition?"

"No, sorry. It's the surgeon in me. I don't

mean to pry, Marcus," Victoria said. "I'm just curious to meet the woman who landed you."

"We were broken up at the time," Alexis said quickly. "He didn't know I was pregnant and I didn't know he was having a kidney removed. Sort of like a secret baby kidney thing."

She was grasping at straws and thinking back to one of Pepper's favorite tropes or whatever she'd called it. It was from the book that had spawned Pepper's bright idea and led Alexis to Marcus, which had then led her here to lying to two amazing surgeons she really admired.

Victoria laughed. "Stranger things have happened. I thought we could have dinner out on the terrace. You two make yourself at home. Matthew, I need help in the kitchen."

Marcus placed his hand at the small of Alexis's back and guided her out to the private terrace. His touch was reassuring and it calmed her nerves.

Alexis took a seat at the table. This house was in the heart of Charlotte Amalie, but it was so quiet. It was peaceful.

"Good save," Marcus whispered, sitting next to her.

"I didn't know we'd get questioned so thoroughly."

"Neither did I. I mean, I knew there would be some questions, but not like that. I'm sorry."

"No, it's fine. They care for you. It's nice."

Alexis wished someone would care for her that much too. She was a bit envious.

"Still…"

"I know!" she exclaimed and they both laughed nervously.

Matthew appeared then with a tray of iced tea.

"It's sweetened," he said. "I've had iced tea that was just cold tea and it's not my favorite."

"Sweet tea is great. Thank you." Alexis took the glass and took a sip. It cooled her down and her frayed nerves, which were on edge, relaxed a fraction.

"So if you don't mind me asking, how far along are you, Alexis?" Matthew asked.

"We do mind," Marcus said, firmly shooting his brother a look of daggers.

"No, it's quite all right," Alexis said gently. "I'm twenty-six weeks along."

"So you didn't know you were carrying Marcus's child when you broke up?"

"Correct." Alexis's cheeks heated again.

"The thing is," Marcus interrupted, "I thought she was a fling. She's British and I had no idea she was a midwife and working here."

"I told you all that womanizing would catch up with you," Matthew said, chastising him.

Marcus rolled his eyes. "Whatever, it's fine now. She's more than just a usual fling. She's my wife."

Alexis was shocked by Marcus's words. She had no idea he was a bit of a playboy. It surprised her, but it seemed everything about Marcus did. Then it made her wonder if his charm, his kiss, had all been a part of this seduction game that he clearly liked to play on women who weren't from here.

Was she just another conquest?

You're pregnant and he met you via Chase and Pepper. You're hardly a conquest.

Still, it reinforced how little she knew about Marcus.

"This was different," Marcus stated, and she realized she had tuned out part of their conversation. "I fell in love."

Marcus reached out and took her hand.

Her heart skipped a beat, and there was a part of her that wished a man like Marcus did love her, but it was all a lie. And lying to Matthew and Victoria, dragging them into this made her queasy.

"Can I use your restroom?" Alexis asked, pulling her hand quickly away from Marcus.

Matthew stood, looking concerned. "Of course. Victoria will show you."

Alexis nodded and dashed inside.

Victoria saw her. "Alexis? Are you okay?"

"No. I feel a bit…"

Sick.

Off.

Guilty.

"Say no more. Third door on the left."

Alexis nodded and ran straight there. Once she'd closed the door she leaned against it, taking deep breaths. When had life become so complicated?

Probably when she'd told Bruce she was pregnant and he'd turned his back on her. That had led her here to the United States Virgin Islands. An escape to paradise. It had worked almost too well as now she didn't want to go back.

She had made friends here. She'd begun to truly live, free of the specter of the pain of what happened with Bruce looming over her…

* * *

"What do you mean you're pregnant?" Bruce asked.

"Isn't it wonderful?" she asked, excited.

"No. It's not. Alexis, we've been through so much because of the infertility issues."

"I know that was difficult, but I'm pregnant now. This is what we wanted."

"I've changed my mind."

She felt like she was going to be sick as the words sank in. "What?"

"I've never wanted children, and I've met someone else who feels the same."

"You've moved on? But how? When?"

Bruce sighed. "Does it matter? It's over, Alexis, and I don't want anything to do with the baby."

It had shaken her. She'd given her heart to Bruce and then he changed his mind and moved on so quickly, as if their marriage meant nothing. How could someone do that? She'd been so angry.

All she could think about was her baby and keeping it safe.

So she left Bruce and England behind.

How could she trust Marcus when he bounced from woman to woman?

She couldn't.

As soon as she had her green card and the marriage ended, she'd never have to see Marcus again.

"Alexis?" Victoria asked, knocking gently. "Are you okay?"

"I'm fine." Alexis opened the door and found Victoria was standing there with a cup of what smelled like warm ginger.

"It's tea. When I get nausea, it helps settle my stomach."

"Thank you." Alexis took the cup. "It's been a long day."

"Not exactly how you planned to spend your wedding night, huh?"

Alexis smiled. "It's unconventional for sure. How far along are you?"

"Only eight weeks," Victoria said. "Still worrying about everything. Babies were never part of my original plan and I don't know much about them, to be honest. I'm a transplant surgeon, and my rotation through obstetrical surgery was short-lived."

"I'm a midwife, so if you have any concerns, I'd be more than happy to help."

Victoria smiled, her dark eyes warm and friendly. "I hear you're a fantastic midwife."

"Who told you that?"

"Chase and Pepper. I was Jonas's surgeon. They tell me that you're familiar with sickle cell anemia?"

Alexis nodded. "When I was a student, I spent a month in Kenya where I learned from an amazing teacher who had not only studied it, but also fought it herself. I wanted to help in any way I could so learned as much as possible. Not so long ago that disease was a death sentence."

"Well, if you're twenty-six weeks, then you'll deliver way before me. I'll stick with Dr. Baxter for my prenatal care, but I will call you if I can't get through to her."

"Anytime. I'm glad to help."

"It'll be nice for my child to have a cousin so close in age though. I had no family growing up."

"None?" Alexis asked.

"I grew up in the foster system. My mother died when I was ten. Never knew my father. There was no one else. I was alone."

Alexis swallowed the lump in her throat. Now she felt even worse for dragging Matthew and Victoria into this deception. Alexis's baby wasn't related to Victoria's and so they wouldn't be cousins.

"Well, enough of this maudlin talk. Let's

have a nice dinner," Victoria said, taking the empty cup from Alexis.

Alexis put on a brave face, but she still felt awful for lying to such nice people. This was not her; she wasn't a liar.

Victoria and Matthew were the type of couple she would like to have as friends. Even, perhaps, as family.

By the time dinner was over it was too late to sail the *Tryphine* home to St. John, so they decided to try out their soon-to-be living arrangements. Tonight would be a good test run. Marcus only hoped he could make Alexis feel comfortable.

He had been worried about her when she ran inside earlier. She looked so upset, but when she came back with Victoria she was calmer, and they had an enjoyable dinner all together. Marcus had given Matthew heck for grilling them, but Marcus also saw Matthew's point—a spur of the moment marriage was so unlike him. Especially when he'd spent years saying he was never going to settle down.

It's for Pepper and Chase.

Chase owed him big time.

Alexis had leaned her head against the window and was snoozing. She looked so peaceful. Almost like an angel.

Get ahold of yourself, man.

He parked the car at the marina lot and reluctantly woke Alexis up.

"Sorry," she murmured softly.

"No need. It's been a long day."

He helped her out of the car and down to the *Tryphine*. He always had his guest berth set up, just in case Jonas came out to stay, so that was a blessing. He wouldn't have to go digging for extra bedding and it was ready for her.

"This can be your room."

"It's lovely. Thank you." Alexis sat on the edge of the bed.

"Are you all right?" he asked.

"How do you mean?"

"I was worried when you ran inside."

"I was feeling ill. Victoria gave me some ginger tea and apologized for so many questions."

"My brother did go over the top," Marcus groused.

"It wasn't just that," she said softly.

"Oh?" he asked, squatting in front of her.

"You never told me you were such a ladies' man before."

"Does it matter?" he asked.

"I suppose not."

Only he could tell by the edge in her voice it did.

He sighed and ran his hand through his hair. "After my fiancée left, I really didn't ever want to settle down. Flings with tourists was the easiest option. They didn't stick around and I didn't get attached. It was perfect, but I haven't done that in a long time. When my godson, Jonas, got sick and needed a kidney I focused all my energy on that. Chase, Pepper and Jonas needed me. You're not cramping my style or anything. There hasn't been a fling like that for close to a year."

Alexis smiled. "I know I'm sort of invading your life."

Marcus leaned forward and smiled up at her. "I like the company."

And he did.

It wasn't just the fact that he had been busy helping out with Jonas. He was also just tired of the pursuit. He was tired of the casual dating, but he was terrified of trying for anything more. He didn't want his heart broken again.

It was too painful.

"Thanks again for all your help today," she said, tucking an errant strand of blond hair behind her ear.

"No problem. Get some rest now. Doctor's orders! We have to hit Immigration early tomorrow."

Alexis nodded. "Aye-aye."

Without thinking he stood, kissed the top of her head and then quickly left her berth. Why did he keep forgetting himself around her? What was this hold Alexis had on him? He noticed her purse had fallen over on the galley counter, and her baby's ultrasound picture had slipped out.

He picked it up so it wouldn't get ruined and saw the name typed on the image.

Baby Olesen.

His heart stopped for a moment as fear overcame him, followed by sadness, because the baby wasn't his. All he wanted in that moment, staring at that picture, was to be with her and be there for the baby whose real father had been a fool and thrown it all away.

CHAPTER SEVEN

ALEXIS STARED UP at the ceiling of her berth on the *Tryphine*. She was exhausted, but she couldn't sleep. She couldn't help but think about where she was and how this was certainly never part of the plan. After what had happened with Bruce, she never thought she would be married and living with a man again.

When she first agreed to this marriage of convenience, nothing in her life was supposed to change. But now everything was changing.

Throwing back the covers, she grabbed the robe that Marcus had lent her and left her berth. She just needed some air and the baby was kicking her, zooming around as if in response to her sleeplessness and everything that had happened in the last twenty-four hours.

A drink of water would help calm everything down. She made her way to the galley and flicked on the light, jumping when she saw Marcus sitting at the table, staring out of the windows.

"Alexis?" he asked. "Are you okay?"

"Just restless. I can't sleep. The baby is kicking me. Why are you up?"

"I can't sleep either. Of course, I don't have the excuse of being pregnant, so I don't really know why I'm still wide-awake."

"Do you mind if I join you?"

"Not at all."

Alexis took a seat across from him and sipped her water as she stared out the window. The city of Charlotte Amalie was lit up, and off in the distance she heard the sound of a horn of a much larger ship, out on the sea.

"It's always louder here off St. Thomas," he mused. "It's why I prefer St. John and my small marina outside of Cruz Bay. I have had offers to open a general practice here, but I don't care for the hustle and bustle."

"I like the quiet too. London was always so busy. I much prefer the country."

"I've never been to London," he said, leaning forward. "What is it like?"

"Rainy," she teased, and he smiled. "Seriously it's a wonderful place. So many old buildings and full of history, but also modern. It was just too…crowded for me."

It also reminded her of her years married to Bruce and how unhappy she'd been. Although the city wasn't to blame for her marriage failing.

"I worked in San Diego for some time. It was too crowded for me as well."

"How did you end up in California?"

"There was no medical school here when I was studying, so I had to go to the mainland. Matthew went to New York, but I preferred the West Coast vibe."

"And what is the West Coast vibe exactly?" she asked, her curiosity piqued.

"Surfing? Avocados?" he offered, teasing.

Alexis chuckled. "Really? That's how you sum up your life in California?"

"Surfing is fun. You should try it."

"Can't really do that in my condition."

He glanced down at her belly and smiled warmly. "No, I suppose you can't. When is the baby due?"

"I think my official date is October 30."

"Almost Halloween."

"I suppose it is. I never thought about it."

"You were the one that had an affinity to

Sleepy Hollow. Please tell me you won't call the baby Ichabod."

Alexis started laughing uncontrollably. "No, I'm not that obsessed with the story."

"Good. I like the way you laugh," he said softly.

"It's easy to laugh with you."

Which was true.

She couldn't remember ever laughing this way with Bruce before. Why was it so easy with a man she barely knew? Probably because there was a part of her that felt she knew him better than she had ever known anyone before. It was a little unnerving to think about.

"Come on," he said, suddenly getting up.

"What?" she asked.

"We're going outside. Maybe some fresh air will help us sleep." He held out his hand.

She knew she should just head back to the privacy of her own berth, but she ignored that niggling little thought and took his hand, completely trusting him as she stood up and followed him out onto the top deck of the *Tryphine*.

The air was definitely cooler outside, and she took a deep breath of the salty air, blowing in off the open sea. Just like the marina in Cruz Bay, the masts of the other boats in the marina were lit up with strings of light.

And the lights of the city of Charlotte Amalie illuminated the side of the hill that the city was built on. It was magical and they stood there, quietly looking up at the clear night sky where a few stars were starting to twinkle. Only, she found she wasn't interested in the stars tonight. She couldn't take her eyes off Matthew.

Her heart began to beat a bit faster, and her body heated at the thought of him being so close. Her husband.

He's not, though. Not really.

"It's a shame," he murmured.

"What is?" she asked.

"The city light drowns out the night sky. Sometimes I take a short sail to St. Croix and just watch the sky on a clear night like this. Once you're away from all the light pollution the stars are endless, like a sea of lights, and for moment I feel like one of those ancient mariners, navigating by the sky."

"I would like to see that," she murmured.

"Would you?" he asked.

His blue eyes were twinkling, and that half smile made her swoon.

She blushed, thankful that he couldn't see her heated cheeks in the darkness. "I would."

She was angry at herself. She shouldn't be considering making plans with a man who wasn't hers and wouldn't ever be hers. Alexis just couldn't bring about the notion or the idea to be with a man, to seriously and really be with a man, who would eventually leave her and her baby.

Maybe her heart could take another bout of heartbreak, but she wouldn't put her unborn baby's heart at risk.

She didn't want that for her child.

A tear slipped down her cheek as her thoughts overwhelmed her.

"Alexis?" Marcus whispered, turning her to look at him. "What's wrong?"

"Just thinking about…thinking about my baby and worrying."

"Worrying about what?" he asked softly.

"The future." She sighed. "I thought that I could do this on my own, but Victoria told me what happened to her and… I guess I'm letting my overactive imagination get away from me."

Marcus wiped the tear from her cheek, and she was embarrassed to be crying in front of him. Her mother told her to never cry in front of anyone because it showed weakness.

Alexis swallowed the hard lump in her throat, trying to swallow down the rocks of emotion that were welling up inside her so that she wouldn't appear weak in front of Marcus.

"I'm sorry," she said, trying to smile. "It's silly."

"It's not. Not at all." And he pulled her close, wrapping his arms around her, holding her. She leaned her head against his warm shoulder and let him hold her. She closed her eyes and felt all that worry and stress just dissipate.

She liked the way that she felt in his arms.

It felt right.

Even though it was so wrong. Even though her heart was at risk.

Even though it couldn't or wouldn't last.

Marcus couldn't sleep. He never particularly slept well when he was moored off Charlotte Amalie, but what added to this insomnia was that Alexis was on the *Tryphine* with him.

Usually when he had a woman on the *yacht* sleep wasn't involved.

His dalliances were just that.

Once it was over, the woman usually returned to her hotel or her cruise ship. They didn't sleep at his place. The only woman he'd ever shared a bed with and slept next to was Dawna. She'd been the only woman he trusted enough to do that with and look where that had got him.

He still wasn't sure what had possessed him to ask Alexis to live with him.

He'd thought that with her in the next berth, it would be fine.

Instead, he couldn't stop thinking about her.

Marcus didn't want to spend his night tossing and turning, so he got up to stare out the window and then she'd come out of her berth wearing his big blue terry-cloth robe. Her hair was a mess, and there were dark rings under her eyes as well.

The way she'd tied the robe accentuated her pregnant belly, and he found her completely enchanting.

And that was the problem.

When he was with her, it was so easy to get lost.

To get wrapped up in her.

And now, as he held her, he didn't want to let her go.

Except that he had to.

She wasn't his.

"Thanks," she murmured as she stepped out of his embrace. The moment she left his arms, he felt lonely and he wanted to pull her back.

"No problem. That's what friends are for, or I guess friends slash husbands." He grinned and she smiled.

"I suppose so and yes, I guess we are friends, aren't we?"

"Exactly. No more of this stranger talk. We're new friends. Isn't there an old saying about making new friends and old ones are like leather or something?"

Alexis chuckled softly. "It's 'Make new friends, but keep the old. One is silver and the other is gold.' No leather involved."

"Leather sounds more daring I would think." He winked, which made her laugh again.

"I'm also worried about tomorrow," she said.

"The meeting with Immigration? Yeah, I am too. I hate standing in lines on the best of days, but it'll go well. We'll follow all the rules and fill out all the paperwork. It'll be fine. We don't make a fuss, we don't draw attention to ourselves and everything should go smoothly, right?"

He had a bad feeling that by uttering those words he was sealing his own doom by taunting the universe and karma in such a way.

"Right. Well, I should try and get some sleep. Good night, Marcus." She leaned over and kissed him quickly on the cheek. It sent a rush of heat through him and he caught her before she could leave, tipping up her chin to kiss her lightly on the lips.

Wanting more but resisting.

He could see the pink flush in her cheeks as she opened her eyes when he pulled away.

"Good night, Alexis."

She nodded once before hurrying away.

Marcus turned to look back out at the water, his blood racing and his heart in very serious danger of falling for a woman that he couldn't possibly have.

CHAPTER EIGHT

THEY WERE EARLY to Immigration, but still ended up stuck in a line to file their paperwork. Marcus was trying not to yawn too much, but he hadn't had the best sleep last night with Alexis being in the next room. So close, yet so far away.

All he could think about was Alexis and how much he wanted to have a real wedding night with her.

Last night had been wonderful. It was so great being with her and with Matthew and Victoria. It felt natural. Like they were meant to be a real family together.

He wanted more. Only he couldn't have more. What if the biological father of Alexis's baby came back? He didn't know how long they had been married, but they had been together by choice.

There was love.

He remembered when he'd been in love with Dawna. He had been so happy.

So clueless.

And he couldn't let himself fall for another woman who potentially might leave him for another man because it had hurt so much when Dawna left him.

He thought his heart had hardened since then, and yet when he was with Alexis, he felt like his heart was softening.

It scared him.

The immigration process went as well as could be expected, and they didn't say much to each other as they headed outside and returned to the boat to sail back to St. John. There were a lot of things to do, like move Alexis onto the *Tryphine*.

Which meant, probably, many more sleepless nights.

As they were leaving, Marcus spied a heavily pregnant woman who seemed to be struggling up the steps to the government building. He glanced over at Alexis, who was watching the woman very closely.

"She looks like she's in pain," he said. "And her belly is quite low. I dare say that baby has dropped."

"I'll be right back," Alexis murmured. She

veered right over to the struggling pregnant woman and asked, "Do you need assistance?"

The woman was sweating. It was hot out, but she was perspiring profusely. It looked like she was struggling to even take deep breaths as she gripped the handrails.

"I'm okay… I…no, I'm just having really bad heartburn, but I have some…paperwork," the woman panted.

Alexis motioned to Marcus to join her.

"Ma'am, I'm Dr. Olesen and this is Alexis, who is a midwife and nurse practitioner. I think we need to get you inside."

The woman nodded, not fighting. "I'm Jill."

"Jill, how far along are you?" Alexis asked as they helped her into the building.

"Forty-three weeks. A touch overdue," Jill panted.

Alexis and Marcus shared a look.

The woman was more than overdue, and he had a feeling that this baby was going to be born in the government building. As they brought Jill through the doors and approached the metal detectors, the security guard stood to meet them.

"We need a room, a first-aid kit and please call an ambulance," Alexis said firmly.

The guard nodded. "You can use the empty first-aid office at the end of the hall."

As soon as Marcus and Alexis had helped Jill into the room, her water broke.

"Oh, my God," Jill said, her voice shaking.

"I think your overdue baby is on its way," Alexis said.

Marcus helped Jill lie down on the nurse's couch and turned to Alexis. "What do you need?" he asked.

"First-aid kit, blankets, gloves."

Marcus made his way to the cupboards and was relieved to find everything Alexis had listed. Today was supposed to be simple. They were going to file their paperwork and then head back to St. John. Turned out nothing was ever easy for the two of them.

He grabbed the supplies he needed and headed back to where Alexis was examining Jill.

"How is it going?" Marcus asked, as he handed gloves to Alexis.

"She's ready to give birth. This one should go fairly smooth."

"What can I do?" Marcus asked.

"She's jaundiced," Alexis whispered. "Check her blood pressure."

Marcus nodded, pulled on some gloves and

got out a blood pressure cuff and sphygmo-manometer.

"Jill, is it okay if I check your blood pressure?"

"Sure," Jill said, wincing and breathing heavily.

Marcus took her blood pressure and it was higher than it should be, even considering the fact that Jill was stressed and in the middle of contractions. He checked her eyes and saw that they were yellowish. She was definitely jaundiced.

"Jill, have you been having pain in your upper abdomen?" he asked.

"Yes. I always thought it was labor, but every time I went to the general hospital in my small town I was sent home."

Marcus palpated, and she flinched when he touched where her gallbladder was.

"How's it going, Marcus?" Alexis asked.

"Tenderness under her right rib. I suspect cholestasis."

"What's that?" Jill asked, panicked.

"Your gallbladder. You might have a stone or an infection. It explains the pain."

"Oh, God," Jill moaned. She was sweaty and clammy.

"Your baby will be…" Alexis trailed off.

"What's wrong?" Marcus said quietly as he knelt beside her.

"The baby is breech. You need to help me when she pushes."

"Tell me what to do."

Alexis nodded. "I need you to press here when I say so."

Marcus put his hand on Jill's stomach where she'd indicated.

"What's happening?" Jill cried.

"Your baby is breech. We're going to try and help her out. It will be a bit uncomfortable but just for a moment."

"Okay." Jill whimpered.

Alexis was waiting for the next contraction, and Marcus waited for Alexis to tell him when to help.

"Now, Marcus," Alexis commanded.

Marcus helped push down on Jill's abdomen as the mother-to-be weakly pushed.

"Push hard, Jill!" Alexis shouted. "Come on, push. Push!"

Jill cried out and delivered her little girl, breech, as Marcus watched in awe. The little girl cried lustily, but Jill didn't respond and Marcus turned to find Jill was unconscious.

"Jill?" Marcus called.

Alexis dealt with the baby, cutting the cord. "I've got the baby."

Marcus checked Jill's pulse. It was choppy, and she was unresponsive. He was worried her gallbladder had ruptured.

He was angry at the emergency room doctors at the small hospital she went to for not checking other symptoms when she was having pains. They'd looked at her pregnant belly and dismissed her.

Now she was sick and would need surgery.

Thankfully, the paramedics arrived just then.

"Patient is Jill. Just delivered a female infant breech and had upper right quadrant pain, with jaundice. I suspect cholestasis. Her blood pressure is high, and her heart rate is dropping."

The paramedics started an intravenous line to get fluids and antibiotics into her, and Alexis handled the baby as the second ambulance crew arrived and brought in an incubator to transport the newborn safely.

"Make sure to take them to Ziese Memorial Hospital," Alexis said. "Let Dr. Miriam Baxter know the baby was born breech and at forty-three weeks."

The paramedics nodded and had it under

control as Alexis and Marcus stood back to let them do their work.

As they escorted Jill and her newborn safely to the ambulance, Alexis let out a breath of relief.

"We make a pretty good team," she remarked. "She was so weak I was worried about losing them both. I don't know what would have happened if you hadn't been there to help."

"I'm annoyed her pain was passed off as labor. Though I have been told that gallstones are often worse than giving birth."

"Hopefully a woman told you that. If a man did, they don't have a comparison."

Marcus grinned. "It was a woman."

Alexis sighed as they cleaned up. "Why is it when we do something important to make our marriage of convenience official something like this happens? Are we tempting fate?"

"We're cursed," Marcus teased. "I forgot to tell you that."

A smile played on her pink, delectable lips that he was now very familiar with. "Perhaps."

They finished cleaning up the best they could—the rest would have to be done by the janitorial staff—and they left the government building.

"I say we head back to St. John," Marcus stated.

"Yes. I have to check on Pepper and get my glucose tolerance test done tomorrow."

"How are you feeling today?"

"Frazzled, but okay. I'll be glad when we're back home."

She had said the word "home" so casually, but it made his pulse race and his stomach twist. She was going to be living with him.

His home would also be hers and the baby's. He swallowed the lump that had formed in his throat. "And we should move your things onto the *Tryphine*."

Alexis paused. "Right. I forgot about that."

"It's safer, just in case someone comes calling."

He was worried about her moving into his space. Especially since he hadn't slept well last night. They left the building and headed back to the marina. Thankfully, it didn't take much for Marcus to release the *Tryphine* from its moorings. In fact, his incision site was feeling much better. He hoped he was finally on the mend after the domino surgery.

The only way to get his mind off Alexis

was to return to his practice, and he was eager to get back to work.

Alexis sat on the deck near him as he headed out onto the open sea.

She was smiling, and as he watched her, he couldn't help but smile too. He had always loved sailing, but Dawna didn't like being out on the water. He should've seen it as a sign they weren't compatible, but he had been so blinded by love.

And honestly, now, being with Alexis, he was beginning to question what he had ever seen in Dawna.

It was a short ride to St. John, and as he pulled up to his mooring he found Chase was waiting at his berth.

Alexis frowned. "I hope nothing is wrong with Pepper."

"Doubtful. He probably just wanted to know how it all went. We were supposed to return last night."

Alexis chuckled. "I'm sure Pepper is dying to know what happened."

He laughed. "No doubt. She probably forced him to come here."

They both laughed at that, because they both knew Pepper so well.

As Marcus pulled up to his berth, he tossed

a rope to Chase so his friend could help him dock the boat. Once the *Tryphine* was secured Chase helped Alexis then Marcus down onto the dock.

"So?" Chase asked. "How did it go?"

"It's all done and I'm moving in," Alexis said brightly. "How is Pepper?"

"Uncomfortable," Chase answered.

"I should go see her," Alexis said.

Marcus nodded. "Remember to take it easy yourself."

"I will. I'll see you later."

Marcus watched her go, and he let out a breath he didn't realize he had been holding in.

"So why didn't you come back last night?" Chase asked.

"My brother," Marcus responded.

Chase laughed. "Oh, I see."

"Alexis is moving in with me."

Chase raised his eyebrows. "So she said, and I have to say I'm kind of surprised."

Marcus shrugged. "Moving in makes sense. We're married. By the way, you owe me big."

"Is it really that bad?"

No.

"Yes." Marcus grinned.

Chase laughed. "You're a liar. I knew when

I saw Alexis that you two would hit it off. She's your type."

"How? She's not the type of woman I usually go for."

"I know. You avoid women like Dawna."

"Alexis is nothing like Dawna."

"She's smart, intelligent and brave," Chase countered.

Chase wasn't wrong, but there was a huge difference between Alexis and Dawna. Alexis wasn't calculating or cold. He hadn't noticed it when he had been so in love with Dawna, but she was career and money driven to such a degree that it didn't matter who she hurt to get what she wanted. Alexis was the opposite. She was willing to do whatever it took to take care of her patients, even going as far as to marry a stranger.

There were similarities, of course, but Alexis was so much more than Dawna was.

Even in such a short amount of time, he could see it.

"You know I'm right," Chase told him.

Marcus rolled his eyes. "Don't let it go to your head."

Alexis changed her clothes and had something to eat before she headed back to the clinic to see Pepper. She was sure Pepper would have a lot of questions. In fact, she was sure that everyone at the clinic would probably have a lot of questions about her sudden marriage to Dr. Marcus Olesen.

Alexis cleaned out her purse and found the picture of the ultrasound. She hadn't looked at it since Dr. Baxter gave it to her as she had been so overwhelmed with everything that had followed yesterday. She smiled as she looked at her little baby. The one she had been longing for, for so long.

When she and Bruce went through all those treatments, they had taxed her emotions. Injections, painful procedures, heartache and loss. She had almost given up hope.

At least Bruce had given her this. Alexis touched the ultrasound, and then she noticed the name typed on the top in bold white letters.

Baby Olesen.

She took a deep breath, her hand shaking. It made sense that Dr. Baxter had assumed Marcus was the father. Still, it made her upset to see that name, and she didn't want Marcus to feel like he had to be a part of her baby's life.

What man would want to raise another man's baby? She shook her head, annoyed she'd let her mother's voice inside her head. Alexis knew plenty of men who would step up. Family wasn't just blood, after all, but there was no denying that Marcus didn't love her or her baby.

They didn't have a relationship. Their marriage wasn't real. The only reason Marcus was in her life, or on her baby's ultrasound picture, was because of Chase and Pepper.

There was a knock at the clinic door, and she tucked the picture away.

"Come in," Alexis called out, hoping her voice wasn't shaking.

The door opened and Pepper came in, her smile wide as she waddled into the room.

"You're back!" Pepper exclaimed.

"I am."

"Did everything go okay?" Pepper asked, closing the door.

"It went fine. I'm more concerned with how you're feeling."

"I'm okay. I've had some swelling."

"Swelling? Where?" Alexis asked.

"In my feet and ankles. Not sure if it's my sickle cell disease or pregnancy."

"Let me see," Alexis said gently. Pepper sat down on the exam table, and Alexis examined the swelling. Then she took Pepper's temperature and discovered that Pepper had a low-grade fever. "You have a fever."

Pepper sighed. "I know. I'm getting close to term, so I thought the pain might be that... I was hoping it was just pregnancy."

"Have you been drinking enough water?"

"I'm floating," Pepper replied sarcastically.

Alexis smiled. "You need to consider bone marrow transplant when this pregnancy is over. For your sickle cell disease."

Pepper nodded. "I know. It's so expensive though, and I have a rare blood type just like Jonas. It's hard to find a match. We're also still paying off Jonas's surgery."

"Well, from what I hear, there's a world-class transplant surgeon in Charlotte Amalie who would help if you asked."

Pepper blushed. "I know that. The domino saved Jonas's life, and I completely trust Victoria. She didn't even charge her fee for the surgery. The bill is just for the hospital stay."

"Well, we'll discuss it more after the baby is born. For now, let's measure you and I want to listen to the baby's heartbeat."

Pepper laid down and Alexis measured her. At eight months Pepper was measuring small, likely because one of the complications of sickle cell disease and pregnancy was preterm birth and low birth weight. The swelling and fever were concerning, though.

It was the kind of potential complication that had made Alexis so determined to stay here and watch over Pepper.

She helped Pepper sit back up.

"Everything is going well. Drink water, rest and that will help with the swelling. You should also take acetaminophen."

Pepper nodded. "I will. So tell me about the wedding."

Alexis chuckled. "What is there to tell? We dressed up, went to city hall and the judge had a stroke after he married us."

Pepper's eyes widened. "Is the judge all right?"

"Last I heard he was."

"Then what happened?"

"We went to the hospital with the judge, and I ran into Marcus's twin and accidentally broke the news of our marriage, not knowing that the man I thought was Marcus was actually Matthew."

Pepper laughed. "Oh, poor Matthew!"

"We ended up making plans for dinner, but I got a little ill and I had to be checked up on by an OB/GYN at the hospital."

"Are you okay?" Pepper asked, concerned.

"I may have gestational diabetes. I have been so preoccupied I didn't get a glucose tolerance test when I was supposed to."

"You need to take care of yourself," Pepper said firmly in her best mom voice, which Jonas had once told Alexis scared him senseless.

"So Marcus said. Medical professionals are the worst patients."

"I can see that." Pepper stood up slowly. "You need to take care of yourself too. After all you've been through…"

Alexis hugged her. "Thank you for your help to keep me here."

"Anytime. I need you, I trust you and I feel safe with you," Pepper said earnestly.

Alexis's heart soared. This was why she did what she did. This was why she loved being a midwife and a nurse. "Try to get rest, Pepper."

"You as well."

"I have to pack up my belongings and move to Marcus's boat."

Pepper cocked an eyebrow. "You're moving in with Marcus?"

"We are married. I know it's one of convenience, but we do have a pretense to keep up."

Pepper grinned. "Of course, you're just

'keeping up appearances.' Sure. Well, I'll leave you to it."

There was something about the way she grinned. As if she knew how Alexis was struggling with her feelings, her attraction to Marcus.

Alexis wasn't worried about moving in with Marcus though. She had slept quite comfortably on the *Tryphine* last night. In fact, it had been some time since she had slept so soundly. It was probably because she felt safe with Marcus.

It unnerved her how comfortable she was with him.

CHAPTER NINE

"How much stuff do you have?" Marcus asked as he carried another box from her small temporary room that the clinic had provided, into her berth on the *Tryphine*.

She couldn't quite believe that she was moving in with him, but the place she had lived at the last four months had been temporary lodgings. If she wasn't planning to stay here because of Pepper and her pregnancy, she could actually be packing to head back to London.

And she was thankful that she could stay on because of Marcus.

The clinic was thankful too, but she still had to empty the room for another nurse or midwife.

Actually, after she delivered Pepper's child, she would have to form her own practice as the government-funded health clinic she'd been working at only offered temporary placements designed to entice new professionals to stay on in the islands.

It had certainly done the trick with her.

The point was, her contract at the clinic would soon be up, and she would have to figure out how she was going to fund and open her own clinic here.

You could ask your new husband to work with you? Or maybe see if there's an opening at his practice?

She shook that thought away. Even though she'd like to work with Marcus, she couldn't ask that from him. He'd already done more than enough to help her by marrying her.

"Hey, I had to move my whole life here as I sold my flat when I took this position."

Marcus set the box on the floor. "I'm glad there's no furniture, but I have to ask one thing."

"Oh?"

"Do you collect rocks?"

She gave him a light punch to his shoulder. "Very funny."

"This is the last box. You're all moved in."

Alexis sighed and sat down on the bed. "It feels weird."

"Hey, I haven't lived with anyone for a very

long time. You're not the only one slightly freaked out about this joint venture."

"Did you live on a boat in California?"

"No. My ex-fiancée didn't like the seafaring life. I was definitely landlocked."

"Would you ever go back to being landlocked?" she asked.

He cocked an eyebrow. "Already complaining about my living arrangements, eh? Trying to get your husband to buy you a castle?"

"Hardly," she replied. "I was just curious. Just trying to get to know you better."

He smiled that half smile she loved so much, and there was a devious twinkle in the blue eyes. "Well, if I ever planned on settling down for real, then I suppose that living here on the *Tryphine* would be tight quarters."

"Just a bit, but I get the appeal of it."

He cocked an eyebrow. "Do you?"

"Of course. You mentioned that you were able to stargaze when you traveled to St. Croix. I'm envious of your freedom to move around these islands."

"Well, the *Tryphine* can't go everywhere. There are some small cays, inlets that she can't get to, which is why I have a small dinghy. It gets me into some hidden places."

"Hidden places?"

He nodded. "Now that you're moved in, why don't we take the *Tryphine* on a short jaunt to other side of the island? I can show you a hidden waterfall that I found. It spills out into a pool and trickles out into a lagoon and into the ocean. Are you up for some gentle adventure?"

Her heart skipped a beat. "I am for sure!"

"Let's do it then! Secure your boxes and then meet me up on deck."

"Aye-aye, Captain."

He chuckled and disappeared back to the upper deck.

Alexis's heart was racing. She certainly wasn't expecting a trip, but she was excited all the same. It would get them away from Cruz Bay and all the lies they'd been having to tell.

And she would love to see a hidden tropical waterfall.

She secured her boxes and made sure everything was safe and sound before she headed up on deck. When she got there, Marcus was talking to someone on the pier. His arms were crossed and his brow was furrowed.

Alexis's heart sank.

Oh, no. It's Immigration.

That was her first irrational thought, but then she got ahold of her panic before it ran away from her and waited out of sight for Marcus to finish his conversation.

Marcus clapped the man on the back and nodded before heading back to the *Tryphine*.

"Is everything okay?" Alexis asked.

"Minor delay. I hope you'll be okay with it."

"Sure, what is it?"

"That was Jem. He's one of the owners of the marina, and one of his sons was working in the back room cleaning fish and sliced open his hand. They really don't want to take him to the hospital, and they were hoping that I could give the lad a quick suture."

"Do you need my help?" she asked.

"I thought you would never ask!" He grinned. "Let me grab a suturing kit and my bag, then we'll head over there."

"Sure."

Marcus was back in a few moments with his bag and what he needed to tend to Jem's son. He took her hand, almost like it was natural, and they walked down the gangplank to the small house where Jem lived.

He was waiting in the small fish-cleaning shack that was on the dock.

The moment Alexis got close, she got a whiff of the fish and her stomach turned.

"You okay?" Marcus asked. "You look a little bit green around the gills."

"It's the fish smell."

"Well, we'll bring the boy out here." Marcus set his bag out on the clean picnic table. "Jem, this is my wife, Alexis. She's a nurse."

Jem nodded. "Pleasure to meet you."

"Can you bring Henry out here? I think it's better we suture him up away from the scales and the fish parts."

Jem grinned. "Of course, Dr. Olesen."

Marcus laid out all the equipment and handed Alexis gloves. She took a seat on the opposite side of the table, because she knew that she would have to help keep the little boy calm.

Jem walked with Henry out of the fish hut and the poor boy had tears streaming down his cheeks. His hand was all wrapped up.

"Henry, lad, what happened?" Marcus asked.

"I cut myself cleaning a snapper." The boy sniffled, giving Alexis side-eye.

"Oh, that's my new wife. Her name is Alexis and she's a nurse, so she's going to help me today, okay?"

Henry nodded and sat down next to her. She rubbed his back.

"Can I see?" Marcus asked as he laid out a drop cloth.

Henry nodded and laid his hand across the sterile cloth. He was wincing.

"You're being awfully brave," Alexis said encouragingly.

"You are," Marcus agreed as he unwound the bandage. "Ouch. Nasty cut, but we'll take care of this. I promise."

Henry nodded and kept his eyes closed.

"I'm going to give you a quick, tiny shot to freeze everything," Marcus said. "Is that okay?"

"Yep," Henry said. As the little boy leaned against her and she continued to rub his back, her heart melted at his bravery. Stitches were never fun, but he was doing so well. And Marcus was so gentle and careful with him.

She watched Marcus in awe as he carefully irrigated the wound on the boy's palm. Marcus talked Henry through the whole thing, making jokes and telling stories as he stitched up the boy's hand. And when it was all done, Alexis bandaged the wound to keep it safe.

"There, that wasn't so bad, was it?" Marcus asked.

Henry opened his eyes and stared in disbelief at his hand. "No, it wasn't, Dr. Olesen."

Marcus grinned. "Why don't you go lay down for a bit? Get out of this heat and rest."

Henry nodded and ran back into his house.

"Thank you two so much," Jem said in relief. "I really appreciate it."

"Anytime." Marcus pulled out his prescription pad. "I'm going to write him a prescription for some antibiotics and painkillers, and I'd like to check on his stitches in a week, if you don't mind."

Jem nodded and took the paper. "Can I pay you, Dr. Olesen?"

Marcus shook his head. "Nope. I'm not supposed to be working right now and Henry does provide me with fresh fish, so we'll call it even."

Jem smiled. "Thanks, Dr. Olesen."

Marcus wrapped up the waste and disposed of it in a garbage bin. The needle he dropped in his portable needle waste container.

"You were so gentle with that little boy," she said in awe.

"It's what I do. Henry is a good lad. Sorry we had to delay our little trip."

She took his free hand. "Don't be sorry. It

was a pleasure to work with you again, even if I didn't do much."

"You bandaged that wound so nicely, and you were emotional support to Henry. That's worth a lot to me."

Her heart skipped a beat as they walked hand in hand back to the *Tryphine*. In that small moment she wished that she was really his wife and not just a fake one.

Even though he much preferred to have the sails unfurled, especially on a bright sunny day like today, Marcus still couldn't manage to get the sails out on his own. But the trip to the little island that was on the far side of the island of St. John, almost to the border of the British Virgin Islands, would be a short trip thanks to the engines on his boat.

Alexis was sitting close to him and drinking in the sun and the wind.

She seemed to enjoy the sea as much as he did.

Another thing to like about her.

Alexis was not making it easy for him to keep his distance from her.

It didn't take long for him to find the small cay. It was rare that anyone came up here because it was so close to the international border, but as long as they stayed on this leeside of the island, they would be fine.

"This is it?"

"It is. See all those other large islands in the distance?"

"I do."

"That's the British Virgin Islands."

"They're so close."

"They are, but if you end up on the wrong side of the border during this green card application, we're toast."

"Noted," she said.

He let down the anchor and then kicked the ladder down. The little dinghy that he used was waiting, and Marcus climbed down first to help Alexis.

For being more than halfway through her pregnancy, she was quite agile. And as he waited for her in the dinghy, he couldn't help but admire her bottom.

"Are you there?" she asked anxiously, dangling her foot down, searching for a foothold.

"I am." He reached for her, enjoying the feeling of holding her in his arms again. "Trust me. I have you."

Alexis let go and he helped her down into the dinghy, holding her so she wouldn't fall. She was laughing and a bit out of breath.

"I don't know how I'll manage to get back up there again," she panted.

"Oh, didn't I tell you I'm leaving you here?"

"Really?" she asked in disbelief.

"Yes. Much like Bluebeard locked his wives away in a castle, I'm confining you to this paradise."

"Yes, but didn't Bluebeard murder his wives because they peeped in his locked room?"

"The point is, it's about confining the wife," he teased, helping her sit down in the dinghy.

"Well, now that you've told me your plan, I can foil it. I do know Krav Maga. I can render you helpless and confine *you* here to the island."

He laughed and untied the small boat, sitting beside the outboard motor. "Clearly I didn't think this all the way through."

He guided the boat from the small cay into the lagoon, past the small grove of mangrove trees and into the taller trees of kapok and turpentine. The sunlight filtered through the leaves, and the water turned from the aquamarine blue of saltwater to clear fresh water as they slowly wound their way through.

It wasn't long before they heard the roar and the rush of the small waterfall that trickled from farther up the side of the island.

Marcus pulled the boat over and jumped out into the water. He pulled the dinghy on the shore and then helped Alexis out.

"This is amazing," she whispered.

"Take off your shoes and we can wade it in it. It's quite shallow."

Alexis kicked off her sneakers and he took her hand so she wouldn't fall on the slippery rocks. She clung to him as she navigated away from the shore into the knee-deep pool that flowed from the waterfall.

He should let her go, but he found that he couldn't.

"This is gorgeous. How did you find this place again?" she asked.

"Just on one of my jaunts. Being on my own, I had some time to explore. That was before my surgery."

"Well, I'm glad you found it." She tilted her head. "What kind of tree is that?"

He looked to where she was pointing and saw a tall tree that had yellow gray bark and spines. "Ah, that's is a sandbox tree, or a 'monkey no climb' tree. You would not want to touch that bark and get a spike in your skin."

She laughed nervously. "I'll take your word for it."

He wrapped his arms around her, just like

he had done last night when they had stared out at the few stars over Charlotte Amalie. When she had been so tiny in his robe.

His pulse was racing.

It was just them, the trees and few birds that were squawking in the canopy above them.

"I'm glad you brought me here," she whispered. "This was a nice distraction from work and worry."

"I'm glad."

All he wanted to do was kiss her.

If she was anyone else, he would, but Alexis wasn't just anyone. She was a temptation and he wanted to indulge. It was then he felt a poke. His eyes flew open and he looked down.

"Your baby kicked me!"

Alexis chuckled. "Yes. I suppose so. You're the first person to feel the baby kick, besides me, that is."

"Can I?" he asked, gesturing toward her belly.

She nodded.

Marcus reached down and touched her gently. There was another little poke, much like a finger, and he couldn't help but smile in delight at that little life inside Alexis letting him know that it was there.

"It's amazing," he murmured.

"It is." She took a step back and looked a bit worried.

"What?" he asked.

"It's nothing. I'm glad you're involved but…"

"I know, Alexis. The baby isn't mine and I know there is a time limit to this whole arrangement, but after this is all said and done we can still be friends, can't we?"

She smiled weakly. "Sure. Of course."

Alexis walked away from him then, wading farther toward the waterfall, and Marcus took a deep breath. He was treading on dangerous ground.

He had to be more careful.

He was in danger of losing his heart not only to Alexis, but also to the possibility of being a father to a baby that wasn't his.

CHAPTER TEN

ALEXIS HADN'T SEEN much of Marcus since she'd moved in and they'd spent time at the secret waterfall. It had scared her when he held her in his arms and reveled in the feeling of the baby kicking. She had been longing for a moment like that to share with someone she loved, but she didn't have Marcus.

And even though she had loved every second of it, she had to protect her baby.

They had headed back to the *Tryphine* and Cruz Bay in silence, but as soon as they got back to the marina Marcus was his old self again. He was acting like nothing had happened, and it was probably for the best.

Really? It's for the best?

They'd tried to settle into some kind of existence together in tight quarters. Having been cleared by Victoria to return to work, he was now back to his practice and after her glucose tolerance test, she had been taking it fairly easy. A lot of the time that mean she went to bed early after a busy day at work.

They had been sort of living in tandem for the last two weeks, and she was finding herself missing him. That short time they had spent together after they were married had been one of the best times of her life, but she also liked this daily routine that she had fallen into with Marcus.

Bruce and she had worked so much, and she couldn't remember missing seeing him as much as she missed Marcus's company. It was nice to talk to someone, to share her day. Especially someone who was interested in her work.

She missed their long talks, missed working with him.

When they'd helped Jill give birth at the government building, Alexis had felt like they'd made a good team.

He was a good partner.

And also a playboy, remember?

From what Matthew had said, she knew Marcus was the type who bounced from woman to woman. Even though he said he hadn't done so in a year, she found it hard to believe that he wouldn't eventually go back to that lifestyle. Why was she falling for the wrong man again? Bruce had been the wrong man, she clearly saw that now, and Marcus, with his penchant for flings, was also obviously the wrong man, yet her mind and heart didn't want to believe that was true.

Alexis stared out of her office window. All she could see was the market. It was busy and the sun was shining. She smiled to herself despite her worried thoughts. She as so lucky to be in paradise.

Her phone rang.

"Alexis Martin speaking."

"Alexis? This is Dr. Baxter calling."

"Yes, Dr. Baxter. How can I help you?"

"I have the results of your glucose tolerance test."

"Oh?"

"It's negative. You don't have gestational diabetes, but you still need to take it easy."

"Thank you, Dr. Baxter."

"I'd like to see you in a couple of weeks for a follow-up ultrasound."

"Sure. Email me sometime and I'll fit it in."

"Very good. Take care, Alexis."

Alexis hung up and was absolutely ecstatic. She decided to go for a walk to clear her head, as she didn't have any more patients for the afternoon.

She made her way out of the clinic and toward the market, soaking in the sun and enjoying the breeze. This was a paradise and she didn't want to leave. For the first time in a long time she was happy with her life.

She couldn't remember being this happy before.

As she glanced across the market, she saw Marcus kneeling next to a little boy who was crying and clinging to his mother. She watched in wonder as Marcus tended to a wound on the little boy's leg. He was so gentle and kind as he cleaned and bandaged the wound.

Her heart melted watching him. The little boy smiled as Marcus finished and stood. Then Marcus rubbed the child's head before turning around to pick up his medical bag.

Maybe he wasn't the cad that she'd assumed he was. People could change, couldn't they?

Marcus looked up and when he saw her, he smiled warmly, like he had been expecting her. It made her heart skip a beat.

"Hi," Marcus said.

"Hi, yourself," she said brightly.

"What're you doing out here?" Marcus asked.

"No patients this afternoon. I thought I'd take a walk, maybe buy some fruit to celebrate."

"You got your green card?" he asked, with what sounded like hope in his voice.

He wants out of the marriage already.

"No, sorry. It's way too early for that."

"Then what was the good news?" Marcus asked, not picking up on her disappointment that he was obviously very eager to get out of their arrangement.

What do you expect?

"I don't have gestational diabetes, but I do have to have another ultrasound in a couple of weeks and Dr. Baxter still wants me to take it easy."

"Take it easy. That's simple enough."

"Is it?" she asked.

"My parents are still on their yearlong world cruise. Usually Matthew and Victoria go and check on my parents' home on St. Croix, but how about we go there for a visit? They have a pool and there's a private beach."

"That does sound relaxing." It really did. She could do with a day by the pool. When they had gone to that private little waterfall, she had desperately wanted to peel off her clothes and take a swim, but the water was so shallow and so she hadn't been able to.

A day of swimming was just what the doctor ordered.

"So let's go."

"Now?" she asked.

"Why not? The *Tryphine* is always ready to go out for a spin."

"Okay, but how far away is St. Croix?"

"Just over an hour. Usually people fly or take a ferry, but we're not so locked in by schedules if we sail ourselves. How about you grab some things for dinner and I'll make arrangements? I'll meet you at home in a hour?"

"Home?" she asked, her heart skipping a beat.

"The *Tryphine*." He grinned.

"Yes. Of course." She nodded. "I'll go to the market and see you in an hour."

Marcus nodded and continued toward the marina, his bag swinging by his side. Even though she probably shouldn't go with him to St. Croix, she was looking forward to the outing. There may be no future for them, but why couldn't they be friends?

She had put her trust in him so that she could get her green card and stay in this place she loved so much. This place she wanted to make her home and raise her child in. And though she was beginning to care for Marcus, it was worth it if it meant she could stay here.

Alexis picked up some fruit and some sandwiches and carried it all back to the *Tryphine*.

Marcus was getting the boat ready. "Did you get something to eat?"

"I did. Did you tell Matthew we were headed there?"

"Yes. He's busy this week, so he's very grateful we're going to check on the house."

Alexis boarded and took the bags to the galley. She put the food away and then headed back up on deck where Marcus was getting some things ready.

"We're going to sail. There's a gorgeous wind today."

"Have you been cleared to sail?" she asked.

Marcus grinned, those blue eyes twinkling. "I have. Sort of. I'm fine."

She crossed her arms. "You're fine?"

"Perfectly."

"So, you're going to sail?"

"Yes, we are."

"We?" Alexis gasped.

"Yes. Nothing strenuous, but we can do this together."

"I don't know how to sail." She laughed nervously.

"I'll teach you."

"You really want me to help you with this?"

"I do," Marcus said happily.

"I don't think this is the wisest idea."

"You told me you wanted to learn how to sail, that you liked to be at sea, and the only way to learn is by doing."

"If you say so."

"What is with the apprehension?" Marcus asked as he released the moorings.

"I'm not the most graceful. My mother enrolled me in a dance class, and they asked me to leave after a couple of weeks because I kept taking out other dancers doing a simple pirouette."

"Well, there are no pirouettes or twirls here. I'll use the motor to get us out of the marina, and then we'll release the sails."

Alexis nodded nervously as Marcus started the engine and the *Tryphine* slipped away. It was a beautiful day, and there whitecaps out on the turquoise sea. There were other boats on the water, and she was excited for the trip and the chance to see St. Croix.

As they cleared the marina and headed out

on the open water, Marcus stepped away from the wheel. "Alexis, take the wheel."

"Me?" She gasped.

"Yes. You."

Alexis stepped up to the wheel and her hands shook as she wrapped them around it.

"Keep her pointing west."

Alexis nodded as Marcus untied a knot and the *Tryphine's* white sail unfurled, flapping in the wind before catching and snapping taut, blinding white against clear blue sky.

She laughed. Joy was bubbling through her as the *Tryphine* conquered the waves and the wind whipped her in the face. Marcus tied off what he needed to and joined her back behind the wheel.

"You're headed north toward the mainland."

"I thought I was going west."

Marcus stood so close behind her she could feel the heat of his body on her back.

It caused her own blood to heat and she leaned closer. His arms came around her, resting his hands over top of hers. Her breath caught in her throat at his touch, and her pulse thundered in her ears as he guided her hands, gently urging her to turn the wheel.

"This way is west," he whispered against

her ear, causing a zing to go down her spine and heat to pool between her legs. Her body was responding to him being so near, and she wanted to give into what she wanted.

And what she wanted was Marcus.

It's the hormones. You're twenty-eight weeks. This happens to a lot of women.

And now it was happening to her. Not surprising, given that her fake husband was one of the most handsome men she had ever seen. Lothario or not, she was completely attracted to him.

She wanted him.

And her body was telling her to indulge.

She cleared her throat and shrugged. Marcus stepped back and went to adjust the boom.

"You're doing great," he remarked. "Now that you're actually going in the right direction."

She laughed. "Thanks."

Marcus had missed her this last week, but he was so glad to be back at his practice and had been hopeful that his work would keep his mind off her.

It hadn't.

Instead, it had reminded him of her. She was such a talented midwife. So confident and knowledgeable. When he worked in his practice, he was all alone. He had a call service and no office. He traveled clinic to clinic and never usually had a reliable nurse.

Working with Alexis was like a breath of fresh air. He missed it, and for one brief moment, he wished they could form a practice so they could work together all the time. He wanted more than just a work relationship though. Even though they had only seen each other in passing these past two weeks, it had felt like home every time he was with her. Like they were supposed to be together.

He was glad they both had the afternoon off. It was chance to get back out on the water and spend time alone with her.

No other distractions.

Alexis had a bit of a struggle with steering. He went to help her, and instinctively he reached out to put his arms around her. If felt so right to be so close to her. Her hair smelled so good. Her body was so soft against him. He wanted to stay there with her pressed against him.

She was so soft.

So warm.

Then she'd tensed, and he realized he had taken it too far. She wasn't interested in him.

Even though he was very interested in her. Attracted to her.

He wanted her.

It scared him how much he wanted her. It had been a long time since he'd wanted a woman like this. The flings were fun, but not completely overpowering. They ran their course, and then he moved on to the next conquest.

Alexis was different.

And for one fleeting moment, right here, right now, he didn't want their marriage to end. He wished it was real. He wished his heart wasn't so closed off.

Alexis did a good job and listened attentively as he pointed out various parts of the *Tryphine* and the sail.

Soon enough St. Croix loomed into view.

Marcus stepped to the wheel. "I'll take over. My parents have a private mooring near their beach."

"They have a private beach on St. Croix?"

"My parents are quite wealthy."

"Quite might be an understatement."

Marcus snorted. "Yes. Just wait until you see their castle."

"Castle?"

"That's what my father likes to think of his home. Bigger is always better to him."

"Bigger isn't always better though," Alexis said.

He smiled. "Agreed."

At the private mooring, his father's boat, the *Freja*, which was a replacement for the *Tryphine*, was in dry dock. As Marcus approached the pier, one of the local workers came out to help.

Alexis was staring at the *Freja* in awe.

"Why pay for a round-the-world cruise when you have that?"

Marcus chuckled. "That's my father. He doesn't want to do all the work for the whole year the cruise would take, and he always needs the best and biggest. I think he's compensating for a poor childhood."

"Was it tragic?" Alexis asked.

"No. Just cramped. He has a lot of siblings. Maybe that's why two was enough for my parents."

His father liked to show off, but he was also generous with his money.

"Colin," Marcus called out to the employee.

"Dr. Olesen, glad to see you again. I haven't seen you since your brother's wedding."

"I've been recovering. It's good to see you too, Colin."

Colin finished up and Marcus helped Alexis down. She was staring in awe at the cliff, which was topped by the house. Or the castle, as his parents like to call it.

"That's going to be quite the walk."

"My father keeps a couple of golf carts for just such an occasion. It's a steep climb, and he's not much of a climber."

Marcus found the golf car waiting, so they both got in. The cart lurched and Alexis cried out, screeching and then laughing. Then he managed to start it properly and tried to remember how to drive the blasted thing.

"Hold on," Marcus shouted over the engine as he took the winding back road up to the house.

Alexis gasped as they came closer. "It's beautiful!"

"It is. It's a great place to spend family time. Victoria and Matthew were married here shortly after the domino."

"I can see why they chose it."

Marcus parked the golf cart, and he opened the back gate that led to where the infinity pool clung to the edge of the cliff, next to the pool house.

"I figure this is a good enough place to have a relaxing afternoon."

"It's perfect."

"You can change in the pool house. I'm going to go for a swim."

"Excellent idea." Alexis made her way to the pool house as Marcus went inside and headed straight for his old bedroom. His parents insisted that Marcus and Matthew keep a stock of clothes there so they could come whenever they wanted, but Marcus suspected that his mother, who tended to baby him a bit, really didn't want an empty nest. Marcus didn't like to be coddled and had rebelled when he was a young man.

He wanted to forge his own path, which was why he went to California instead of New York like Matthew. Of course, he'd been in love, which was another reason why he didn't follow his twin. He loved California and he just wanted a simple life.

Only Dawna had a different idea. She'd wanted a different life, so he'd started to transform himself to fit that vision. Now he realized how unhappy that life had been. Being with Alexis had made him realize that he had been mourning a life that was never his design.

What he had to figure out now was what to do. What he wanted. Dawna had hurt him, and he never wanted to feel that again. He didn't want to transform his life for someone who was going to hurt him.

He finished getting dressed and headed back out to the pool.

Alexis was already there lying on a lounge chair. She wore a black one-piece, and he could see the swell of her abdomen clearly. The curves of her body. She was glowing and absolutely stunning.

Probably the most beautiful woman he had ever seen.

Alexis took his breath away, and he was in severe danger of falling for her.

A woman who didn't want him.

Marcus came out of the house, and Alexis tried not to stare at his broad, bronzed chest. There was a faint pink scar on his side from the domino surgery. She still couldn't believe he gave his kidney to a stranger. He was so unselfish.

There were so many things she admired about him. He made her weak in the knees and as she watched him swim, all she could think about was his arms around her. How safe he made her feel when she had been vulnerable.

How good he made her feel.

She thought of his lips on her and the kisses they'd shared. Her body heated and her stomach did a flip. Alexis couldn't remember the last time she'd wanted a man this much.

Why couldn't she indulge?

All her life she had always followed the rules and never her heart. Everything was thought through ad nauseam.

She trusted her gut, but never this instinct. Never pursued her desire.

Not in this way.

What would be the harm just this once?

"Are you coming in?" Marcus asked, treading water.

She nodded and slipped off her lounger to slowly walk into the saltwater infinity pool. The water was warm, and she didn't hesitate to sink into it. Marcus swam over to her. His blue eyes were twinkling as he wrapped his arms around her, pulling her tight against him.

"Is this relaxing enough?" he asked.

"Very," she murmured, her heart racing, and she wrapped her arms around his neck, leaning in closer. She couldn't help herself and kissed him lightly on the lips, as she had done before.

"I have missed you the last couple of weeks. I know we're strangers in a way, but I missed having talks with you. It's been nice sharing a home with you. I've been in the Virgin Islands for some months, and I didn't realize how lonely I was."

"I've missed you, too," Marcus whispered huskily. "I've gotten used to having you around."

She kissed him again. Deeper this time, letting him know just how much she wanted him. This marriage might be fake, but what she was feeling for Marcus was very real.

And for once in her life, she wanted to act on instinct. She wanted to feel.

Even though there was an end date to all of this, she wanted to feel some kind of passion in her life before the baby came.

It had never happened to her this way before. She desired Marcus like no other man.

She craved him. She was treading on a dangerous path by kissing him, but she didn't care in this moment. All she wanted was Marcus. His hands skimmed over her, and a tingle of anticipation ran through her.

"You're so beautiful," Marcus murmured as he kissed her again, making her blood heat.

"I want you," she said, surprised at how uninhibited she was when she was around him.

Marcus kissed her again. "Are you sure?"

She nodded and kissed him again. "I'm very certain. I just want to be with you, Marcus."

Marcus lifted her up and carried her out of the pool. He carried her to the outdoor shower, and her body thrummed as he ran his hands over her and touched her intimately as they rinsed away the saltwater and peeled off their swimsuits. It was just them, nothing between them anymore, and he pulled her tight against him, kissing her neck.

Warmth spread through her veins as his lips moved down her body to her breasts. Alexis cried out at the sensation of his tongue on her nipple. It was pure pleasure. Her body was so sensitive to his touch, and he continued to run his hands over her before stroking her between her legs, bringing her to the edge before backing off, leaving her desperate for more. She wanted him. She needed him.

He picked her up again and carried her into the pool house, straight to the bedroom.

He laid her down and kissed her again. She arched her back, silently begging him to take her.

She wanted more.

So much more.

Their gazes locked as he entered her and then paused.

Emotions overcame her and a tear slipped from her eye.

"I'm sorry," he whispered, brushing it away. "I'm hurting you."

"No. You're not. Don't stop," she murmured. "Keep going."

Marcus tenderly touched her cheek. "As long as I'm not hurting you."

"You aren't." She kissed him again.

If she was hurt, it wouldn't be his fault. It would be hers for letting herself fall for him.

Marcus nipped at her neck and began to move slowly, gently.

All she wanted was Marcus to take her.

Possess her.

She wanted him deeper and she wrapped her legs around his waist, begging him to stay close, but her belly was making it difficult to take him as deep as she wanted while she was lying on her back.

"Hold on," she murmured.

Marcus withdrew and she rolled on her side, her back to his chest. Marcus's hand slipped under her leg as if he knew exactly what to do. He draped her leg over his and moved his hand to her breast as he entered her again. Her body lit up as pleasure washed through her. She had never felt this way before.

She was falling in love with Marcus.

Alexis shook that thought away. There was no room in her life to love a man who didn't want her. She wasn't going to put her heart at risk again. So she was going to savor this moment, and she was going to hold on to this memory long after their marriage had ended.

Marcus quickened his pace and she came, crying out as heat washed through her.

Absolute pleasure.

Marcus soon followed and then gently eased her leg down.

"Alexis," he whispered, pulling her body closer to him.

"I know," she replied, trying to catch her breath, floating down from the high.

She wanted to tell him that she was falling in love with him, that she wished this marriage was real, that she wished she had met Marcus a long time ago and that she wished she hadn't been so hurt and he hadn't been so scarred.

Their timing sucked, but at least he had come into her life.

Even just briefly.

Marcus held Alexis close to him. He was spooning her, and her luscious bottom was snuggled up against him as she slept. He didn't want to disturb her, but he also couldn't stop touching her. He let his hand lightly touch her belly.

How he wished he could have her and the baby in his life. Try as he might, he just couldn't stay away from her. He was falling hard for her. If he wasn't so scared, he could reach out and just take it. He could have it all, but he wasn't sure if Alexis wanted it.

And that thought scared him.

How could he let her inside his heart only to have it shattered again when she chose someone else? The answer was simple, according to the logical part of his brain: he couldn't. Yet, his heart was begging him to take a chance.

It had taken him so long to mend himself after Dawna. Alexis understood that pain only too well. Her ex-husband had left her for another. But she had picked herself up and moved to a completely different country, starting over.

It made him angry that her ex-husband had thrown her away and that she'd felt she had no choice but to leave home.

Still, what if this Bruce guy wanted Alexis back?

The idea made Marcus angry. Bruce didn't deserve Alexis, but he wasn't going to stand in the way of the child's biological father either.

It made him anxious not knowing if Alexis wanted him, not knowing if her ex-husband might come back into her life. It made him feel powerless, and there was nothing he could do except wait it out. He wouldn't blame Alexis if she decided to go back to her ex-husband, because what did he have to offer her besides a green card?

CHAPTER ELEVEN

ALEXIS WOKE UP from a nap to find Marcus's arms around her. Their bodies were a naked tangle, the sheets damp, but the breezing wafting in through the open French doors was warm. The sun was low in the afternoon sky.

She rubbed her eyes, wondering what the buzzing sound was before realizing it was her phone. She fumbled through her purse and pulled it out.

"Alexis Martin," she said.

"Alexis! It's Chase!"

The panic in his voice woke her up. "Chase, what's wrong?"

"Pepper has gone into labor."

"How far apart are the contractions?"

As soon as she asked that, Marcus sprang up and left the pool house completely naked to go and get dressed.

"Fifteen minutes. You have time to get here."

"I'm on St. Croix."

"Oh… What…? Oh, no!"

"I'm going to get a flight. I'll be there as soon as I can."

"Okay. Hurry."

Alexis hung up the phone and grabbed her clothes, pulling them on haphazardly. The last time she'd checked on Pepper this week she was stable with no signs of preterm labor, and her swelling from her sickle cell disease from a couple of weeks ago had dissipated. That was why Alexis had thought it would be safe to leave the island today.

Apparently, fate had other plans.

Marcus came back to the pool house looking concerned. "It's Pepper, right?"

Alexis nodded. "Yes. I need to get a flight back to St. John."

Marcus nodded. "I have a buddy with a private plane. I contacted him and he's going to take us. We have to drive to Christiansted and meet him at the airport."

"Let's go then."

Marcus led her to a garage and past some expensive and unique cars, choosing instead a beat-up truck that seemed out of place around all the luxury.

As if reading her thoughts, he said, "This is the truck I learned to drive in."

He started the engine, and then they were off on the short drive to the outskirts of Christiansted where Marcus's friend was waiting. The plane was tiny and made her a bit anxious as well as nauseous, but she held it together.

All she cared about was getting to Pepper. Until she met Marcus, Pepper was the first person she'd really connected to since her marriage ended. Her first real friend on the island when she'd arrived. Pepper was the reason Alexis was still here.

It was breaking her heart that she was so far away. She felt like she was letting Pepper down.

Contractions are fifteen minutes apart. There's time.

The flight took under half an hour. Marcus had called Matthew, and he was there waiting to pick them up at the airfield. Luckily, Matthew and Victoria had been visiting to check in on Jonas when Pepper had gone into labor.

When Marcus and Alexis got off the plane, Matthew's face relaxed, his relief evident.

"Thank goodness you're here," Matthew said.

"What's her status?" Alexis asked.

"There's swelling and she's jaundiced. I think it is a flare-up of her sickle cell disease, and I think that's what started her labor. We did start an intravenous line for fluids, but Pepper refuses to leave her home. She wants you."

Alexis's stomach knotted. "Are the paramedics on standby?"

Matthew nodded.

They all climbed into the car and raced over to Chase and Pepper's home. With Marcus following, Alexis made her way to the bedroom, passing Victoria and Jonas, who were sitting in the living room looking very worried.

Chase got up when Alexis entered. She had left a birth kit here for them, and she was glad to see that Chase had already pulled it out.

"Thank God," Chase said.

"I'm sorry I'm late." Alexis washed her hands and checked on Pepper. Her feet were red and swollen, as were her knuckles, and when Alexis took her temperature it was high.

"How far apart are the contractions now?" she asked.

"Five minutes," Chase said.

Alexis felt Pepper's belly. The head of the baby was not where it was supposed to be. Alexis did an internal exam and discovered that the baby was not engaged and was breech. Pepper was not quite fully dilated, so there was time to turn the baby.

If it didn't work, they would have to get Pepper to Ziese Memorial for an emergency C-section. Even then, it might be too late.

"Marcus, we need to give her a dose of antibiotics in her intravenous line. Then, we need to turn the baby. With the swelling she won't be able to deliver this baby breech, and we're running out of time to transfer her to Charlotte Amalie."

Marcus nodded and got what he needed from the paramedics, injecting the medicine into Pepper's intravenous line.

"Chase, keep her calm. We have to manually turn the baby. It will hurt her."

Chase paled, looking frightened.

He was terrified. She was too. Alexis had done this before and it was never pleasant. Now she was having to do it to her friend. A person she cared for deeply.

Pepper was crying from the pain and knowing it was about to get worse broke Alexis's heart. She was glad Marcus was here with her. She trusted his skill, and she needed him.

"Tell me what to do," Marcus said.

"Just follow me. We're going to try an external turn."

Marcus pressed his lips together, and they waited for the next contraction to pass before attempting to move the baby. Pepper cried out in agony as they did so, but Alexis could feel it work as the baby started to turn.

One more turn.

They waited until the next contraction passed.

"Now," Alexis said.

As soon as they turned the baby, Pepper's water broke and the baby descended. Alexis nodded at Marcus. "That will do."

Pepper had fully dilated, and Alexis could now see the baby's head. She took a cleansing breath, very relieved that the procedure had worked and that the premature baby was coming out in the right direction.

"What's happening?" Pepper asked groggily.

"Your baby is coming," Alexis responded.

"Alexis?" Pepper asked, confused.

"Yes. I'm here. Pepper, next contraction I'm going to need you to push."

"Okay," Pepper said with a whimper.

The contraction came and Pepper pushed, screaming as Alexis encouraged her. With each push the baby came closer until, with one last push, the tiny girl was born crying as she entered the world. Alexis felt tears sting her eyes as she held that beautiful baby. Though she had been taught not to cry, she couldn't help herself in these circumstances.

Chase and Pepper were ecstatic.

Alexis cut the cord and handed the baby over, waiting for the placenta to be delivered. There was some excessive bleeding, so Alexis spoke with the paramedics.

"We have to get you to Charlotte Amalie," Alexis said.

"Why?" Chase asked.

"She's bleeding heavily, and we need to treat her for her flare-up of sickle cell disease. Your baby is doing well, but she is early, so I want her checked out by the neonatal intensive care unit."

Chase nodded. "Will you come?"

"We all will," Marcus said.

Chase nodded again. Alexis stood back to let the paramedics load up Pepper and the baby. As she stepped out into the other room, Jonas sprang up from the couch.

"How's my mom?" he asked.

"She's fine. You have a new sister," Alexis said.

Jonas grinned. "Cool."

"We have to take them to the hospital to be checked out, but they're both going to be just fine."

Jonas nodded. "Okay."

"We'll bring him to our place," Victoria said. "You and Marcus can stay with us too. We have room."

"Yes," Matthew said. "I assume the *Tryphine* is still at St. Croix?"

"You assume right," Marcus replied. "Thank you both."

After Pepper and Chase were loaded into the ambulance, Victoria and Matthew drove Jonas to the ferry and Alexis and Marcus walked the short distance. Alexis needed some air.

"You were amazing in there, you know," Marcus said.

His compliment made her blush. "Just doing my job."

They shared a smile, her pulse racing.

"It's been quite a day," he said, staring up at the sky.

"And it's not over yet."

Marcus sat outside on Matthew's terrace. The sun had set. Pepper, Chase and Jonas were at the hospital with their new little girl, Charlotte. Victoria was also at the hospital with Matthew, working out how to convince the board to consider a pro bono bone marrow transplant surgery. If they were successful, they wanted to start the search right away to find a match for Pepper. Victoria had even mentioned grand plans of a database of rare blood types to be matched around the world.

As much as Alexis had wanted to stay with Pepper, she was exhausted and needed rest, so Chase had ordered Marcus to take her back to Matthew and Victoria's place for a shower and a nap.

He went to check on her then, and though he wanted to join her, he knew if he laid down next to her he would want her again. He couldn't quite believe they had made love this afternoon. It had been overwhelming.

He'd been completely lost to her. She had been so soft, so warm and so tight. His blood heated and he took a drink of his scotch, then set the glass down.

What was he doing?

It scared him how much he wanted her. How he wanted to bury himself inside her and claim her as his own. Except there was an expiration date to it all. He had always known it was going to end; he just hadn't considered the possibility of it ending early.

He had collected the mail before they left for St. Croix, and there was a letter for Alexis. It was from England, and Marcus suspected it was from her ex-husband. He knew it was only a matter of time before the other man would want to come back into her life. His fear seemed to be coming true.

She was talented.

Smart.

Beautiful.

What kind of man would want to give that up?

He certainly wouldn't.

He was falling for her.

Actually, he had already fallen for her. Which put his heart in jeopardy once again, because Alexis would definitely choose the father of her baby over the man she was fake married to.

Alexis came out onto the terrace, interrupting his spiraling thoughts. "I fell asleep again."

"It's okay. You had a busy day."

"Where is everyone?"

"Chase and Jonas are with Pepper and Charlotte. And Victoria and Matthew are working to get a bone marrow transplant for Pepper to alleviate her sickle cell disease."

"That's wonderful. That will help."

"It's just you and I here tonight."

"I should be with Pepper at the hospital."

"Why? Pepper and Charlotte are stable and in good hands. You need rest, Alexis."

"She's my patient. And my friend."

"Exactly and as your friend Pepper wants you to rest. She said so herself."

"Fine. You're right. I am tired."

Alexis took a seat next to Marcus.

"You were incredible," he said. "Did I already tell you that?"

She laughed nervously. "I've turned a baby before."

"That's not what I'm talking about."

Pink flushed her cheeks. He knelt in front of her and touched her. She trembled under his caress, and her breath caught in her throat.

Though he shouldn't, he wanted her again. One time wasn't enough.

He wouldn't get her for a lifetime. So he just wanted this small fraction of time with her.

"I want to kiss you," Marcus whispered against her ear.

"Then kiss me," she said.

She pulled him close, and he sank into the deliciousness of her lips. He couldn't help himself when it came to her.

He was lost.

So lost.

He was also terrified of letting her go. He wanted this to last forever, but he didn't know how to make that happen. He could smell her scent, feel the warmth of her body. He wanted to drown himself in her.

"Marcus," she whispered, just as he felt her tears.

"You're crying?"

"I'm overwhelmed," she said. "My mother told me to never cry in front of other people. She said it was a weakness."

"Oh, no. It's not a weakness, Alexis. Far from it." Her skin was so soft as he traced her cheeks. "Never hide your tears from me."

Alexis laid her head against his shoulder and he drank in her scent, that luscious perfume of green tea and jasmine. She deserved more than him. She probably wanted someone better than him, just like Dawna had.

Dawna had found someone better, but he didn't want to think about her right now. He didn't want to think of her ever again.

"Marcus, thank you for being here with me."

"Anytime." He leaned in and kissed her again, just like he'd wanted to do since he woke up and watched her sleeping in the pool house, before the phone rang and all hell broke loose. He was glad that she was there for his best friends.

She fit into his world so naturally.

Before the phone rang he'd wanted her again, but he knew another brief stolen moment would never be enough. Not when it came to her.

"Marcus," she whispered against his lips.

"Alexis, I burn for you."

"I want you too." She kissed him again, hungrily. "I want you so much."

Marcus wanted to take his time with her. He didn't want to rush this moment. It was something he would hold on to for the rest of his life.

He scooped her up into his arms and carried her to their room. He set her gently on her feet, not wanting their connection to break. Not wanting their kiss to end. They made quick work of their clothing. He wanted nothing between them. Just skin to skin again as he made love to her.

She ran her hands over his body. He loved the feel of her touch; it made his skin break out in gooseflesh.

"I love the way you touch me," he said huskily.

"I love touching you."

He touched every part of her. Kissed every inch of her until she was wet with need.

They moved to the bed and settled onto it. He cradled her body from behind, just as before, so he wouldn't crush her. Her skin was soft as silk as he traced her curves. His blood was on fire as he slowly entered her. She was so tight and warm around him.

Alexis moaned.

"Please," she whispered, clinging to him. His hand moved to her breast as he quickened his pace and she came around him, squeezing him. It wasn't long before he joined her.

Nothing had ever been like this with anyone else before. It was overwhelming.

Alexis fell asleep soon after and he stayed

there, holding her, touching her skin. As his hand drifted across her belly, there was a push against him.

It was a kick.

He smiled, keeping his hand still so that he could feel it again.

Another kicked pushed at him.

He wanted to be in Alexis's life. He wanted to be a father to her baby, but he was worried he was not the one she wanted and that one day the man she truly wanted, the baby's father, would come back and his heart would be shattered again.

Marcus was gone when she woke up. He left her a note that he had flown back to St. Croix to retrieve the *Tryphine*.

She was a bit disappointed that he hadn't woken her. She wouldn't have minded sailing back from St. Croix to St. John with him. She cleaned up and got dressed before making her way to the kitchen to get something to eat.

Victoria and Matthew were in the kitchen.

"Good morning," Alexis said.

Victoria smiled. "Good morning."

"How is Pepper's transplant plan going?" Alexis asked.

"We've got it mostly figured out. Now we

just need to take our plan to the board of directors and then find a donor once they approve it," Victoria answered, pouring a glass of orange juice.

"I doubt they'll say no to Victoria. She's quite bossy," Matthew teased, looking lovingly at his wife.

Alexis was envious of their love. She wished that Marcus looked at her like that. What Matthew and Victoria had was real. What she and Marcus had was lust and deception. The love she thought she'd had with Bruce wasn't deep like this. She wasn't sure if she'd ever known what true love really was until now.

"Maybe it has something to do with the fact that I performed an expert and successful domino surgery?" Victoria teased back, leaning over the counter to kiss Matthew.

Alexis wanted this, but she wasn't sure that she'd ever have that kind of connection. That kind of deep love.

"Well, I have to get to work." Matthew kissed Victoria again. "Try to take it easy."

Matthew left, and Victoria poured Alexis a glass of juice.

"Are you okay, Alexis?" Victoria asked.

"Just tired. Twenty-eight weeks and I seem to have hit a wall."

"You're a trooper," Vic said.

"As are you. As a surgeon you must be on your feet for hours."

"Not anymore. Dr. Baxter's orders." Victoria sighed. "Transplant surgeries are quite long, and Dr. Baxter doesn't want me on my feet as I'm an older mother-to-be."

"Transplant surgeons aren't the only victims to taking it easy. Dr. Baxter said the same to me."

Victoria smiled. "I'm glad I'm not alone."

"No, you're not."

"You seem a bit sad today though," Victoria said quietly.

Alexis forced a smile. "No. Not sad."

Which was a lie. Another lie. She hated lying to Victoria. She wanted to tell her the truth, but she was also ashamed that her marriage was fake. That her baby was not Marcus's. What seemed like a simple solution to stay in the country was becoming more and more complicated.

Especially when it came to her heart.

She was in love with Marcus, and though she should've said no to him last night, she couldn't help herself. She had to be with him again. Even if it was for one last time.

It had been so overwhelming. She couldn't

help but cry. She was so overcome with the stress of Pepper's birth, her own pregnancy and falling for a stranger. She was annoyed with herself for being too vulnerable around him.

For letting him into her heart.

What was wrong with being vulnerable?

Alexis took a sip of her orange juice, but she found it was hard to swallow. It was like a rock going down and sat heavily in the pit of her stomach. She was done lying. She had to tell them all the truth, even if it meant that she would have to return to England.

Even if it meant that she would lose Marcus.

Victoria let out a little moan. Alexis glanced up to see Victoria's face had gone ghostly white, and she was gripping the counter as if her life depended upon it. She was swaying back and forth, and there was a fine sheen of sweat on her brow.

"Victoria?" Alexis asked.

"I don't…" Victoria's eyes rolled into the back of her head and she went limp. Alexis had just enough time to leap up and blunt the woman's fall as Victoria fainted right in front of her.

CHAPTER TWELVE

ALEXIS WAS PACING outside Victoria's room. Dr. Baxter was in there with Victoria right now. After she had fainted and came to, Alexis drove her to the hospital and paged Dr. Baxter to come straightaway.

Matthew was in surgery and Marcus was still at sea. It was just Alexis as next of kin, though she wouldn't exactly call herself that.

So instead of being in the room with Victoria, she was pacing and waiting for the answer from Dr. Baxter. Alexis had her suspicions about what could've caused the episode of fainting, but she didn't know Victoria's medical history, and at this point all she could do was speculate.

And with the way she was already feeling—worried and anxious—her mind was racing to a bunch of horrible conclusions, which was not like her at all.

Dr. Baxter finally came out of the room and Alexis pounced.

"How is she?" Alexis asked.

"She's fine. I think given that pregnancy causes an increase in hormones, which in turn increases blood flow, it caused the blood vessels to dilate, which in this case led to the syncope."

Alexis let out a sigh of relief. "I'm glad it's nothing more than that."

Dr. Baxter nodded. "I'm going to keep her overnight for observation anyway. Not that she's too impressed."

Alexis smiled briefly. "I'm not surprised. I keep getting reminded that medical professionals make the worst patients."

"That they do. Speaking of which, how are you feeling? I hope you're taking it easy."

"I am. I'm tired, but I am doing the best I can to rest…"

"And relax. You seem stressed."

Alexis laughed nervously. "Well, it's been a hectic couple of days, what with Pepper Fredrick giving birth early."

"I was told you did an excellent job externally turning that baby, and that you studied the effects of sickle cell disease when you were a student."

Alexis nodded. "I did."

"I'm impressed, Alexis. Truly I am, but you need to take it easy. You're not a diabetic, but your blood pressure is still running higher than I'd like, and I'm concerned about pre-eclampsia."

That sobered Alexis. The only way to cure preeclampsia before it turned into the fatal eclampsia was to deliver the baby. She was only twenty-eight weeks along; it was too soon for her to deliver.

"I promise I'll take it easy."

"Please see that you do." Dr. Baxter left her then, and Alexis ran her hand over her face.

She knew that part of her stress was this fake marriage and all the lying, which meant she knew one very easy way to alleviate the stress. She could tell the truth. She couldn't deceive these people anymore. It wasn't right. She liked Victoria and Matthew too much.

They were treating her like she was family, when she was anything but.

Alexis knocked softly and then entered Victoria's room.

Victoria was lying against the pillows and looked a little bit better than she did before, right when she'd first fainted.

"Your color is better," Alexis said brightly.

"I feel better." Victoria held up her arm to show an intravenous line. "I think the fluid is helping. I was also dehydrated."

"I'm glad to hear you're feeling more yourself." Alexis sat on the edge of the bed.

Victoria cocked an eyebrow. "There's something you want to tell me."

"Yes."

"And I think it's something you've wanted to tell me for some time."

Their gazes locked, and then she saw it in Victoria's eyes. That keen perception. There was no fooling a world-class surgeon.

"You know, don't you?"

Victoria smiled weakly. "I suspected. I know what kind of crazy ideas Pepper comes up with."

Alexis laughed softly. "Yes."

"So tell me. I promise I won't say anything outside of this room."

"I won't hold you to that, but I'll tell you because it's eating me alive and I don't like lying. I'm not that good at it. My work visa was expiring, but Pepper needed me. I understood her sickle cell disease better than any other midwife in the islands."

"Yes. Pepper really did need you."

"She came up with the idea that I should

have a marriage of convenience. Straight out of one of her favorite books."

Victoria smiled, her eyes twinkling. "And Marcus, the ultimate playboy, agreed?"

"You've read the book?"

"I enjoy them." Victoria grinned. "So, Marcus agreed to the plot?"

"He did."

"And the baby?" Victoria asked gently.

"My ex-husband's. We tried for two years to have a baby, went through so many procedures. When I found out I was finally pregnant and told him, I thought he would be ecstatic. I was. It was everything I'd ever wanted, but he'd changed his mind."

"How dreadful," Victoria said softly. "I would've punched him. Did you?"

Alexis half smiled and then shrugged. "No. It is what it is. My mother wanted me to get rid of my baby. She felt it was a hindrance to me finding another husband. I don't have the most supportive parents."

Victoria shrugged. "You know my story. I can relate."

"I do. I'm sorry."

"It's okay."

"I always wanted a baby. Even though my parents were so emotionally distant. My ex signed away his parental rights. He didn't want my child and that was fine. I didn't expect Marcus to claim my baby when I met you, but he did and since then it's been eating away at me. You've all been so kind. I wasn't trying to take advantage of Marcus. I didn't want any of you to get hurt."

Victoria took her hand. "I know. I'm glad you told me the truth. I'm not mad at you. I understand why you did it, and I know things have changed."

"Changed?"

"You love him."

Alexis's breath caught in her throat, and there were tears stinging her eyes. Was she so transparent?

"Victoria?" Matthew stuck his head in the door. "Are you okay?"

"I fainted. Hormones, swollen blood vessels and a wee bit of dehydration," Victoria said. "I'm fine."

Matthew crossed the room and kissed his wife. "You're sure?"

"Ask Dr. Baxter yourself," Victoria said. "Thankfully, Alexis was with me when it happened."

Matthew turned and looked at her, gratitude etched on his face, one so like Marcus's and yet so different. "Thank you."

"My pleasure." Alexis snuck out of the room then, leaving the couple alone. It felt like a weight was off her shoulders, but now there was another issue.

She did love Marcus, but she wasn't sure of his feelings.

Just ask him.

Only, she was terrified to do that. She was so scared of Marcus turning her down like Bruce had. What man, who had made it quite clear that he was a playboy and had no interest in a real marriage, would be interested in a woman who was pregnant with another man's child?

Who would want to take on that kind of baggage?

She wasn't going to force that onto Marcus. She couldn't do that to him precisely because she loved him. She wished her marriage wasn't fake. She wished she didn't have to wait so long to hear about her green card, so that this whole charade could end.

Then Marcus would be free.

Even if the idea of being free of him tore at her very soul.

As she walked down the hall, she looked

up to see Marcus coming toward her. Relief was evident on his face as he approached.

"I got your message. Is Victoria okay?" he asked.

"Yes, she is."

Marcus sighed with relief. "That's great."

Her stomach twisted in a knot, and he picked up on her tension.

"Marcus, there's something that I need to tell you."

"What?" he asked gently.

"I told her… I told Victoria."

"Told her what?"

"About our marriage of convenience and about how the baby isn't yours," she whispered.

"Why did you tell her that?" he asked, pulling her into an empty room and shutting the door so that they wouldn't be disturbed.

"I had to tell them. The guilt was too much."

"Yeah, but now you've implicated them. I didn't want them to know."

Alexis worried her bottom lip. "I'm sorry. They've been so kind, like family. They needed to know the truth about me and the baby."

"Yeah, but they're not your family. They're

my family, and you've put them in jeopardy by telling the truth."

It was like a slap to the face. It stung, and it hurt so much more than Bruce telling her that he didn't want their child. She had thought that Marcus was different.

Clearly he wasn't, and she was annoyed at herself for giving her heart to another man who didn't want her.

Clearly he saw her as just another conquest. How could she be so blind?

"That was not my intention."

"Yet, that's what you did. You weren't the only one taking a risk entering into this marriage. It was a business deal between the two of us."

"You brought your family into this when you didn't tell me you had an identical twin and claimed my child as yours!"

Alexis wasn't wrong. It was ultimately his fault that Matthew and Victoria were in danger.

She was only with him to get her green card, but there was a part of him that had hoped for so much more. Yet it was clear she didn't want him in her life, didn't want him claiming her child. If she did, wouldn't she want to continue the act?

He loved her, but he was so afraid of putting his heart on the line for someone who wouldn't stick around.

It was better that he remained single and live out that life that he'd originally wanted to pursue when he first headed to California, before life became complicated and before his heart was broken.

Even though this hurt, pushing her away was a lot easier than having her stick around and hurt him in the end.

Marcus pulled out the envelope. "This came for you a couple of days ago."

Her eyes narrowed and she took the envelope. "It's from Bruce."

He nodded. "It is."

"Why did you hold on to this?"

He shrugged. "I forgot. Things got a bit hectic."

"You knew it was from my ex-husband, and you kept it from me?" she asked.

"I didn't realize a letter from your ex-husband was so important," he responded coldly.

"Well…it is. It is his child I carry."

"I'm sorry." And he was. For so many

things. He hated hurting her, but it was better this way. Wasn't it?

Alexis opened the envelope, and her expression was unreadable. "He wants me back. Me and the baby."

"So our marriage is over."

She looked up at him. "No. I don't have my green card."

"So what? We stay married until you get your status?"

"We can't get divorced."

He nodded. "I get it. You were only with me so that you could get your green card. I suppose we both got swept up in the idea of having a marriage and family, but that's not what I want. Your ex does though."

"Why?" she asked quietly.

The question caught him off guard. "What do you mean why?"

"Why don't you want a family? What did this Dawna person do to you to harden your heart so much to the idea? You run from any kind of relationship. Isn't that why you only pursue women who have an expiration date? You know in advance when the end is coming so you won't be blindsided."

The truth hit him like a ton of bricks, but he didn't want to hear it. He couldn't hear it.

"I'm not the only one who ran away! You ran from England and took your child away from its biological father; a man you were married to. You said that he was not coming back, but here he is and he wants his child. Now who is the one who is clinging to a fake relationship that has an expiration date? You're just with me for citizenship, and then you'll run back into his arms. Well, I won't stand in the way. We'll be married on paper until you get your green card, but I don't want to be part of your life in the meantime."

Her eyes filled with tears, but she carefully folded her letter and put it back into the envelope. "You're absolutely right. This was a business arrangement, and you lived up to your end of the bargain. So, when the time comes, I'm going to give you your quickie divorce. I will move my things out of your place tonight. You'll hear from my lawyer."

Alexis pushed past him.

His heart was aching.

He couldn't believe he'd let himself be hurt like this again. When Dawna broke his heart, it had reminded him of all those lonely years in boarding school.

Everyone doted on Matthew and his academic excellence, but Marcus just wasn't as brilliant as his brother. He struggled, he acted out, he was the disappointment.

All he wanted to do was return home, but his parents wouldn't let him. They told him that he had to be independent, and he hated that. He was lonely, but he put on a brave face and sucked it up.

He was the only person who had never disappointed himself.

Liar.

Letting Alexis walk away was so hard, but this marriage wasn't real. No matter how much he wanted it to be. He didn't want to fail her. He didn't want to disappoint her, and he didn't want to hurt her child.

It was too much of a risk to everyone's heart.

It was easier to let her go, even though he was being torn up inside and it felt a lot like his heart was on the verge of breaking. He took a deep breath and sat down, dropping his head into his hands. All he wanted was her and her baby, but they were off-limits.

If he lost them, he couldn't go on living.

Except that he had already lost them, if he'd even ever truly had them.

He had pushed them away but it was for the best. Alexis had come here to take care of herself and her child. She didn't need to be shackled to a coward who wasn't sure that he could ever give his heart over completely, because he was too afraid about what the future might hold.

Because he was too afraid of losing any happiness that he might find.

CHAPTER THIRTEEN

IT HAD BEEN two weeks since Marcus had pushed Alexis away. Two horrible, lonely, awful weeks.

Was this really the better way?

He finished tying the knot he was working on and then realized it was completely wrong. His head wasn't in it at all. All he could think about was Alexis. He never stopped thinking about her. When he got back to the *Tryphine* at his Charlotte Amalie mooring, her berth had been emptied out. She was gone.

When he returned to St. John, he discovered she hadn't returned to her dormitory room either. It was like she had faded into nothing. She was gone, and he was worried about her. Worried that she wasn't taking care of herself, that she wasn't relaxing. That he'd broken her heart too deeply. And he couldn't help but wonder if her ex-husband had come back into her life. The thought of the man who threw her away touching her again was almost too much to bear.

Except he had thrown her away too.

Pushed her away, even.

Now he was the fool.

"You're an idiot, you know that, right?"

Marcus looked up to see Matthew standing on the dock of his St. John mooring.

"What?" Marcus asked.

"The knot is all wrong," Matthew said, pointing to it.

"What would do you know about sailing? You hated it," Marcus replied dryly.

"Okay," Matthew said, climbing up on the *Tryphine*. "Then you're still an idiot for another reason."

"Oh?"

"Alexis."

"What about her?" Marcus asked, grumpily tossing the rope down.

"Why did you let her go?" Matthew asked.

"Let her go? What do you mean I let her go?"

"You love her but you pushed her away."

Marcus frowned. "Our marriage wasn't real."

"It may have started that way, but you fell in love with her."

"What does it matter? Her ex-husband is the father of her baby, and he wants her back."

Matthew shrugged. "And what if he does? Is that what she wants?"

Marcus sighed. "It was her ex-husband. She loved him. I'm just the second choice. I'm the man she married so that she could stay in the country. I'm nobody."

"She's not Dawna," Matthew said gently.

"Why are you pestering me about this?" Marcus snapped. "I thought you said you weren't going to try and parent me again."

"This isn't parenting. I want to see you happy, you fool!"

Marcus snorted. "Sure."

Matthew leaned forward. "Look, buddy. I'm going to tell you what you told me when you were recovering from the domino. You told me that Victoria loved me and that I had always loved her. You also called me a chicken for not sticking it out in New York and running away all those years ago. You also accused me of trying to murder you by injecting morphine into your drip, but that's beside the point."

Marcus chuckled. "That's not fair, I was drugged up."

Matthew grinned. "You love her and I dare say she loves you, too."

"Did she tell you that?"

"No, but her actions made it clear that she cares for you. Why else would she tell Victoria the truth? The point is that Alexis cared enough about you and your family to tell the truth. She loves you, and you're too stubborn to see it."

Marcus's heart ached. Matthew was right. He had been too blind to see it.

Too stubborn.

He had fallen in love with her. He wanted to be a part of her life and her baby's life. He was still thinking about the way that little kick had felt against his palm. He was tired of being alone behind this wall that he'd built to keep his heart safe.

He groaned. "I am a fool."

Matthew grinned. "I've been saying it for years."

Marcus rolled his eyes. "Thank you for reminding me who I am, Matthew."

Matthew put his hand on his brother's shoulder. "And thank you for doing the same for me."

"Anytime, brother. There's just one problem."

"What's that?" Matthew asked.

"I don't know where she is."

It had been two weeks since Marcus had hurt her, but she still didn't think that he'd meant to hurt her.

What was he so afraid of? What was *she* so afraid of?

Her mother's voice was still rolling through her head as she mulled it all over while walking the halls of Ziese Memorial Hospital. She missed Marcus. She loved him and with how her heart ached, she realized her love for Bruce had never been the same.

It was so much more with Marcus.

He may have been a lothario in his past, but he was different now, and what they had shared was something deep. The moment she first met him—even though he may have been a stranger—her soul had felt like she had known him for a long time.

And though she wanted him back, she didn't want to put her heart back on the line again.

It was too hard.

And it wasn't just her heart that was in danger, but also her baby's. She placed her hand on her abdomen and felt her baby kick. All that mattered was protecting her child.

Alexis stopped in front of Pepper's door and knocked.

"Come in!"

Alexis entered the room to see Pepper cradling little Charlotte.

"How are you?" Alexis asked brightly.

"Feeling great and eager to go home."

"I'm sure."

"How are you?"

"I've been better." Alexis sat down on the bed to stare at the baby longingly.

"I heard you and Marcus called it off."

"Called it off? It was a marriage of convenience. As soon as I got my green card our deal was going to be over."

"Deal? I think it was more than that."

"What do mean?" Alexis asked, blushing.

"I saw the way he looked at you, and I saw the way you looked at him. You are in love with him and he's in love with you."

Alexis felt tears sting her eyes. "No. He's not in love with me. He pushed me away, and I don't blame him. He doesn't want me."

"Why? Why would you think he wouldn't want you?" Pepper asked gently.

"I'm pregnant with another man's baby."

Pepper shrugged. "So?"

"And my ex-husband wants me back."

"Do you want Bruce back?" Pepper asked.

"No, I don't."

"So what's the problem?"

"Marcus thinks I'll go back to him."

"Have you told Marcus you're not going to?"

Alexis sighed. "No."

"Then I don't see the problem."

"My mother said no other man would want to take on another man's child. I won't put my child at risk of Marcus leaving us one day."

"No offense, but your mother has very outdated views and didn't exactly care for you the way she should have."

Alexis chuckled softly. "She does have outdated views, and you're right. I can see it. I don't think she ever really cared for me."

"They why did you let her into your head?"

It was a good point. She didn't know why she had let her mother's opinion control her actions. She'd worked hard her whole life to keep her mother out, but this one time, when it mattered the most, she'd let her in and ruined something precious as a result.

"You know how I know that your mother is wrong?" Pepper asked.

Alexis brushed away the tears. "How?"

"Jonas isn't Chase's biological son. I was pregnant with Jonas when I met Chase, but Chase didn't care. He became Jonas's father and we became a family. I've known Marcus for a long time. He's had flings, but he was never happy. With you, he was happy. With you, he found love."

Alexis began to cry and she leaned over to hug Pepper.

"Thank you," Alexis said.

"For what?"

"This crazy idea of a marriage of convenience."

Pepper grinned. "See, there's nothing wrong with a good happily-ever-after is there?"

"No. You're right, but that's if I *get* a happily-ever-after. What if I hurt Marcus too much? What if he doesn't want me back?"

"You've got to take the risk. It's worth it, Alexis. It's so worth it."

Alexis left Pepper's room and headed out into the hall. She had to find Marcus and make it right. She had to tell him how she felt about him. She was scared that he might turn her down, but she had to know for sure how he felt.

She walked down the hall, her pulse racing and turned the corner, stopping short when she saw Marcus at the end of the corridor.

He was dressed in a tuxedo, which was the strangest sight.

It made her heart skip a beat.

"Marcus?" she called out.

"You moved away," he said.

"Yes," she replied, her breath catching in her throat as she walked toward him. "I did."

"Where did you go?" he asked, closing the gap slowly.

"Pepper and Chase's. They gave me a room until I could find my own place."

"I went there. You weren't there," he said softly.

"I didn't want to see you."

"I know and that's my fault. I pushed you away. I was jealous your ex-husband had sent you that letter. I thought you would choose him, just like Dawna chose someone else over me."

"I didn't exactly stop you either. I pushed you away, too, because I was scared you would resent me, or resent being hitched with me and another man's child."

He smiled. "I know and I don't blame you. I hurt you, and I betrayed your trust keeping that letter from you."

"I hurt you too."

"Alexis, I love you."

Her heart skipped a beat, and she couldn't help but smile. "I love you, too."

He put his arms around her. "I don't care that the baby is not biologically mine. The baby is a part of you, and I love you. I want you both in my life. I want us to be a family. Do you want that?"

Tears streamed down her face. "I do want that. More than anything."

"So what do we do about your ex and the baby?"

"I told him I wasn't coming back. He was angry, but he doesn't want the child or the responsibility of one without me. He can't be bothered with us, and we'll tell our child the truth about her genetics when the time is right, though I don't think blood matters."

"Our child?" he asked.

She smiled. "Yes. Our child."

"Did you say her?"

"I did. Sorry. Didn't mean to ruin the surprise. Are you angry?"

Marcus smiled and tipped her chin. "I'm

going to kiss the bride now, properly, like I should've done when we were married a month ago."

Heat bloomed in her cheeks. "I would like that very much."

She didn't wait for anyone to pronounce them husband and wife, just wrapped her arms around him and let him kiss her.

When the kiss ended, she leaned her forehead against his, just like she had done when they had been in Dr. Baxter's office and seen their baby for the first time.

"You know, I was worried when I saw my ultrasound picture."

"Why is that?" he asked.

"It had your name on it, and I was worried that you would run then."

"I have a confession to make," he said. "I saw that photo. It fell out of your purse."

"How did you feel when you saw it?" she asked.

"Pride. I've always wanted a family, and I don't care what my family is comprised of. I learned a long time ago, when I met Chase, that family has nothing to do with blood and everything to do with love. And when the baby kicked me for the first time, the night we made love, I wanted to be your baby's father. I still want that more than anything."

"And you're the man I want. You're who we both want." She kissed him again.

"I'm glad," he said. "But we do have a minor problem."

"What's that?"

"As much as I hate to say it, the *Tryphine* is no place to raise a child."

"You're right. So what do we do? Where do we go? My contract at the clinic is up, and frankly I like working with you. I think we make a good team."

"I would love to have a nurse and a midwife as part of my practice. So you're okay staying on the island of St. John?"

"There's no place I'd rather be."

Marcus kissed her again, and they left the hospital hand in hand.

A family.

Finally.

Forever.

EPILOGUE

One year later, St. Croix, Halloween

"HOLD LUCY UP HIGHER, Marcus. I don't want to see your face. I just want to see my sweet granddaughter in her new birthday dress," his father demanded.

"Gee, thanks, Father." Marcus hoisted his daughter, Lucy, who was turning one today, up on his shoulders so that his father could take a photograph.

His parents had returned from their round-the-world cruise just in time for Alexis to give birth to their first grandchild. Four months later, Victoria had given birth to their second grandchild.

Another girl.

Lucy and Ava Olesen weren't exactly twins, but everyone liked to comment that they were as they both had dark hair and blue, blue eyes.

Marcus's parents didn't care that Lucy was not their biological grandchild. They loved her just the same.

The moment that Alexis had given birth to their daughter, which was the most nerve-racking moment of Marcus's life, he'd fallen in love with that beautiful girl who was placed in his arms. The baby that had kicked him for months.

Matthew had been sick with worry when he saw Marcus's haggard expression after the birth, because he had been worried about the same thing happening to him. And the same thing did happen to him.

When Victoria gave birth to their daughter, Ava, he had also been completely enraptured with his little girl.

Their father had seen it as a blessing, and he was the most doting grandfather to ever set foot on the island of St. Croix. He was constantly boasting about his granddaughters, which was why Papa Olesen had insisted on throwing a lavish birthday party for Lucy at the family castle. Another lavish first birthday party was already planned for Ava in a couple of months' time.

"Give her to her papa."

Marcus handed over his daughter to his

father, and the happy little girl laid kisses on her grandfather's face.

Freja, Marcus's mom, came out onto the lawn with the pink-and-white strawberry cake and Alexis followed behind, but she was a bit precarious on her feet. She was pregnant again, and this time it was twins. Three was enough though; Marcus was already drowning in diapers.

Matthew liked to tease him about how Marcus went from gadding about on the *Tryphine* to gadding about the superstore and stocking up on baby supplies.

Victoria was rocking Ava, who was napping, her little birthday hat crooked on the side of her head.

"He really is a great papa," Victoria murmured. "Our kids are so lucky to have them. To have this family."

Alexis sat down next to her. "I agree."

Marcus smiled at both of them and then shared a secret smile with his brother.

"I never thought in a million years that we would be here," Matthew whispered.

"Neither did I."

"I'm glad we are, though."

"Me, too."

And he was. For years he'd dreamed of having a life like this. He wanted big family gatherings, love and happiness. He and Matthew had spent too long competing and bickering; he was glad that they were so close again now. It was a closeness that he had missed sharing with his brother for too many years.

And they finally had it.

It only took the love of two good women to make it happen.

Marcus had moved his practice with Alexis to Ziese Memorial Hospital after Lucy was born as it was easier to go in on the costs of day care with his brother at the hospital and he liked working close to family.

They'd bought a small house not far from Matthew and Victoria in Charlotte Amalie, but they still kept the *Tryphine* for when they wanted to have a private getaway. And he loaned it out to his brother too.

This was what life was all about.

Family, and the love of a good woman.

Marcus sat down next to his wife. "How are you feeling?"

"Bloated," she murmured. "I think this might be my last trip to St. Croix for a while. Dr. Baxter doesn't want me leaving the city."

"I know. My parents will soon descend on the new condo they bought in Frenchtown."

"You can't keep Papa and Nana from the girls," Victoria said.

"Are you guys going to come and watch the birthday girl blow out her candles?" Freja asked.

"We'll be right there." Marcus stood and helped Alexis up.

Victoria slowly stood, trying not to wake Ava, who was letting out a sweet snore.

They all walked over to the table where Freja was lighting the candles. Lucy looked at him and held out her chubby little arms.

"Dada. Want Dada."

"Sorry, Dad. I outrank you."

His father grinned. "As you should."

Marcus took his little girl in his arms as the candles were lit. Even though she was only turning one, Nana had put several on there as a form of good luck.

Alexis wrapped her arm around his waist and laid her shoulder against him.

"Make a wish, Lucy," Marcus urged. "Then blow out the candles."

"No, Dada. You wish."

Alexis chuckled softly. "What're you going to wish for then, Dada?"

Marcus kissed the top of Alexis's head and then his daughter's. "I have everything

I could ever wish for. Come on, Lucy, let's blow them out together."

He leaned over, and he and his little girl blew out the candles.

His heart was completely full.

He was whole.

His brother was whole.

His family was no longer broken.

And there was love in the castle on the hill.

*****

*If you missed the previous story in
the Caribbean Island Hospital duet,
then check out*

Reunited with Her Surgeon Boss

*If you enjoyed this story, check out these
other great reads from Amy Ruttan*

Falling for His Runaway Nurse
Falling for the Billionaire Doc
Twin Surprise for the Baby Doctor

All available now!